Don't Shoot the Gentile

James C. Work

From one writer to
one better writer —
Thank you, John!
Jim Work

UNIVERSITY OF OKLAHOMA : NORMAN

Many, if not all, of the characters and names in this book have been changed to protect the innocence, real or fictional, of persons both real and fictional. Likewise, certain details have been added, omitted, exaggerated, or falsified for purposes of plot.

Library of Congress Cataloging-in-Publication Data

Work, James C.
Don't shoot the gentile / James C. Work.
p. cm.
ISBN 978-0-8061-4194-7 (pbk. : alk. paper)
1. Work, James C. 2. Mormons—Utah. 3. Cedar City (Utah)—Fiction. I. Title.
PS3573.O6925Z46 2011
813'.54—dc22
[B]

2011001194

The paper in this book meets the guidelines for permanence and durability of the Committee on Production Guidelines for Book Longevity of the Council on Library Resources, Inc. ∞

Contents

Don't Shoot the Gentile

Prologue

We enjoyed the pleasant strangeness of a city of fifteen thousand inhabitants with no loafers perceptible in it; and no visible drunkards or noisy people; a limpid stream rippling and dancing through every street in place of a filthy gutter; block after block of trim dwellings, built of "frame" and sunburned brick—a great thriving orchard and garden behind every one of them, apparently—branches from the street stream winding and sparkling among the garden beds and fruit trees.

Mark Twain, *Roughing It* (1872)

The overland stage journey described in *Roughing It* took Mark Twain through Utah where he encountered his first Mormons and rewarded their hospitality by poking fun at their customs. It was the college teaching internship described in *Don't Shoot the Gentile* that took me into Utah and my first encounter with Mormons. Now it's my turn to reward their hospitality with anecdotes about people I met there. The names have been changed, but they will know who they are.

Usually an internship is a formal period of training; in my case it was a potpourri of life lessons so informal as to verge upon chaos. When my wife, Sharon, and I first arrived in the Mormon town of Cedar City, Utah, I was young and unknowing and thirsting for experience; by the time we left I was inebriated with self-confidence and reaching drunkenly for the next rung on the stepladder of academia (though I had not yet mastered the art of metaphor). As far as understanding the culture of southern Utah is concerned, let's just say that I arrived naïve and departed slightly less so.

According to one definition, an "intern" is someone confined to an institution. And confining is what the little village in southern Utah did at times seem. I wasn't alone in thinking so; each time I asked Cedar City freshmen to write an essay entitled "My Hometown" the term "provincial" popped up almost as frequently as the terms "boring," "jail sentence," and "what did I do to deserve this?"

"Intern" can also mean someone who has been sent to some interior location such as an internment camp. With deference to Utah's jaw-dropping scenery, I have to say that sending a native Coloradoan away from the Mile-High State to *anywhere* is tantamount to exile. Or relocation, at least.

Following our return to Colorado, our friends joshed us about having been non-Mormons among the Latter-day Saints. And I'd josh right back, saying that I had been on a mission to convert people to the Word of Jim Beam. Friends would ask how many times per week someone in a white shirt and dark tie pushed our doorbell. Few believed me when I said it never happened. Eighty percent of the residents of Cedar City were either active or recovering Mormons, yet no one ever approached, accosted, queried, or propositioned us. (OK, I was propositioned once, but that was different.)

We wondered at it ourselves. Were all the Mormon missionaries out of town on missions? Was there a community pact to leave the Works to their Presbyterianism even though they were nice young people and it was a shame they were headed for hell? A year after we got there I was told that a young woman named Miriam Angeline Works (1806–32) was the first wife of the Mormons' renowned leader, Brigham Young. However, she died before Brigham met Joseph Smith, the founder of the church, and so she could not have been a Mormon.

Whether or not she was an ancestor of mine I do not know. Either way, it had nothing to do with the fact that in two years no Mormon missionary ever came to our door. The revelation of the real reason came toward the end of our internment in the south of Utah when we found out that of all the non-Mormons in all the Mormon communities, the Works were the *last* ones they wanted to convert.

I will soon describe how my little family and I happened to move to Cedar City in southern Utah. How the *Mormons* happened to get there is more complicated an epic that could (and does) fill volumes.

If any of my history classes explained the settlement of Utah by the Church of Jesus Christ of Latter-day Saints, it must have been a day I was absent. All I learned in high school was that Utah lies west of Colorado, that there is a big lake of water so full of salt you can't sink in it, and that when Brigham Young saw it, he said, "This must be the place." A college history instructor repeated this same store of knowledge, adding (with a wink and a nudge) that people in Utah practice polygamy. I didn't know how one went about practicing polygamy—I figured that after two or three marriages to different people you wouldn't really need any more practice.

I could be wrong about the power of practice, of course. After all, half the population of the globe is still practicing religion. And if the history of warfare is any indication, people need to practice a bit harder. Religious people worldwide kill each other and die over whether you should wear white or black, pray on your knees or on your face or standing up, and how much wealth, territory, and sex you are entitled to by virtue of your chosen sect. Or the sect chosen for you by God.

One feature is so common among major religions that it sounds like one of those archetype things. In one manifestation of the archetype the prophet Muhammad was visited by angels (around 610 A.D.) and wrote a holy book containing the word of Allah and thus Islam was born. But prior to the angel Gabriel giving the Koran to Muhammad, a Hebrew named Abraham got into a covenant with God and began sharing his truth with the Hebrew people, which led to the Torah and the book of Genesis and an outbreak of enthusiastic begetting among Jewish people, not to mention a whole bunch of swordplay and plagues.

While some will say that Buddhism is not a "religion" in the strictest sense of the word, it resembles other religions in that it begins with a young man—Siddhartha—hearing the voice of the Almighty, getting confused, and going off to meditate. Alone in nature he found enlightenment and shared it with lots of followers.

I told you this story would sound familiar, didn't I?

There are dozens of similar instances of mortals who heard God (or angels), took dictation, and after a certain period of meditation went forth and founded a following. The most successful of these in latter days (meaning any time after some previous time) has doubtless been the church founded by Joseph Smith of Vermont and carried forth by Brigham Young, also of Vermont, who led Smith's Latter-day Saints into Utah.

It began something like this:

The angel named Moroni visited Joseph Smith in 1823 and showed him metal plates with strange writing on them. Smith transcribed and translated the writing, which turned out to be a new gospel that he called the Book of Mormon (1830). Smith gathered up some followers (see *The Gathering of Zion* by Wallace Stegner) and they ventured forth to establish their new church in the Far Distant West, which in those days was somewhere around Ohio. The Latter-day Saints were subjected to a series of burnings, lynchings, kidnappings, and torture by people who fervently believed in God, Moses, Christ, and the fellowship of man, but who didn't want anyone to tell them about an angel named Moroni. In 1844, after further violent atrocities by anti-Mormon morons, Smith was murdered while in jail at Carthage, Illinois.

Which is where Brigham Young entered the picture to assume leadership of the Latter-day Saints. Around 1846 Brigham and other survivors of the Illinois massacres started toward the Pacific, mostly to distance themselves from the Atlantic where the Good Christians lived. In 1847 the Saints came to a wide valley and a vast salt sea. When they showed it to Brigham Young, who was sick and delirious at the time, he said, "This is the place," and lay back down (see Ernest H. Taves's *This Is the Place*). Young's followers took this as a sign that they should lay claim to it. Since the water was too saline even for fish and the surroundings were mostly desert or mountains too densely forested to get a wagon through, no one objected.

In 1849 the Mormon settlers declared the existence of the State of Deseret. The U.S. Congress changed this to Utah Territory in 1850. Also known as the new Kingdom of Zion, in 1896 it became the forty-sixth state. The state flourished; the church of Latter-day Saints flourished.

Joseph Smith's revered account of Christ is not unique. Every religion worth its salt has a book containing the history of the tribe along with the rules and recipes for staying on God's good side. In the Church of Jesus Christ of Latter-day Saints the volume contains fifteen books (Nephi, Mosiah, Ether, and so on); two chapters called the "Doctrine and Covenants"; a section called "The Pearl of Great Price" consisting of Joseph Smith's translations of the books of Moses, Abraham, and Matthew; and part of Smith's personal history.

An otherwise well-meaning reader of my manuscript suggested that I explain the Mormon position on alcohol, caffeine, tobacco, and "skirt chasing," issues that have been explained, interpreted, argued, explicated, documented, and debated until the resulting academic volumes now occupy twenty-two and a half feet of shelf space. And that's just in the Denver Public Library.

Let us begin with the least complicated human activity known to man, namely marriage. Joseph Smith was familiar with Shakers (United Society of Believers in Christ's Second Appearing), among whose beliefs was the conviction that the celibate life was preferable to the married state. Reasoning that a church whose members shunned sex would have a limited life span, Joseph sought God's counsel. The message he received is found in Doctrine and Covenants 49:16: "Wherefore, it is lawful that he should have one wife and they twain shall be one flesh and all this that the earth might answer the end of its creation." To me this seems to pretty much sum up the Church's position on "skirt chasing," adultery, and even polygamy. If you want to get into why Brigham Young could have dozens of wives, you'll need to go read about it somewhere else. Period, full stop.

I will now proceed to a topic often related to marriage, namely the use of alcohol. And tobacco. And other stimulants. Doctrines and Covenants section 89 is introduced with a headnote in which Joseph Smith says that "as a consequence of the early brethren using tobacco in their meeting, the Prophet was led to ponder upon the matter."

I infer that Joseph Smith grew sick and tired—mostly the former—from sitting in church meetings with men puffing away on pipes and cheroots until the air became opaque and reeked like smoldering silage. I can sympathize because back in my undergrad days there were no strictures against smoking in classrooms. In creative writing workshops I often had to lean down and look under the layer of smoke to see who was reading.

Joseph Smith sought the counsel of the Lord concerning the burning of tobacco in church meetings. What he received was a set of revelations known today as the Word of Wisdom. The Word of Wisdom says that tobacco leaves can be used as a poultice to heal wounds on animals—and indeed, tobacco has a certain numbing and antiseptic effect—but that it doesn't seem very smart to roll it into a cylinder, stick it in your mouth, and set fire to it.

While the Lord was on the subject, he also gave Joseph Smith a few words of wisdom about alcohol and other stimulating drinks. Drinking wine as a sacrament can be permitted, but "this should be pure wine of the grape of the vine of your own make." What the Saints are really against is drunkenness. And why go to the bother of fermenting grain and distilling it *except* to get drunk? And who (with the possible exception of creative writers) ever accomplished anything worthwhile while intoxicated? The Word of Wisdom says that each grain, like each fruit, is "ordained" for a particular use—but those uses are supposed to be nutritional rather than recreational.

Verse 9 of section 89 says "and again, hot drinks are not for the body or belly." As generations of wise elders pondered the meaning of this they arrived at the natural conclusion that Joseph Smith was referring to coffee, tea, and hot chocolate. After all, what other hot drinks did they have in those days (if we eliminate alcoholic hot cider)? And what do these hot drinks have in common? Caffeine. Caffeine is not specifically proscribed in the Doctrine and Covenants; avoidance of it is a custom born of a human interpretation among a people bound together by common beliefs. Or common sense.

I knew none of these things when I took the job in Cedar City. It may seem hard to believe, but I knew absolutely nothing about Mormons or Latter-day Saints. All I knew was that I had a cushy job in a clean little town surrounded by Kodachrome scenery and populated by hospitable folk who minded their own business and let Sharon and me mind ours.

Mark Twain was twenty-six years old when his California stagecoach made a stop in Salt Lake City. He marveled at the Mormons' clean streets, substantial homes, and the ingenious urban irrigation system.

I was twenty-five years old when I arrived in Utah and saw the clean streets, tidy houses, and the irrigation water sparkling alongside sidewalks and flowing into gardens. Twain was a writer and a Gentile and went on to become famous. I was a writer and a Gentile and I just went on.

Twain said several unkind, exaggerated, and untrue things about the Mormons, but he got at least one fact straight. "Gentiles," he wrote, "are people who are not Mormons."

"Gentile" in Latin is *gentilis*, meaning someone who belongs to a particular tribe or clan. It distinguishes between "them" and "us." The French later used a version of it to refer to the upper class or "gentry." Margaret Nicholson's *A Dictionary of American-English Usage* tells us that Jews used "gentile" to distinguish anyone outside of their tribe. Also according to Professor Nicholson, all non-Moslems in India became known as "outsiders" or "gentiles." This may hold true in the Near East, Far East, and Middle East, but if you let any Moslems or Jews set foot in Utah they instantly turn into Gentiles. If they try to argue about it and point out that they are not Christians, some Mormons will say that Latter-day Saints are not Christians either, although other Mormons profess to be. In Utah, Mark Twain met his first Mormon; it was in Utah that I first met my first Jewish Gentile at a place affectionately called CSU.

It is possible that some readers have never heard the College of Southern Utah referred to by that name. Therefore I will clarify.

The stalwart Cedar City citizens who fought snowdrifts and blizzards to erect the first college building in 1897 christened the place "Branch Normal School" or BNS. I do not know what it was a branch of, nor why they thought it was normal.

In 1913 it became the Branch Agricultural College (BAC), reflecting an elevation in status from "school" to "college" and recognizing an emphasis on agriculture. Apparently the idea of normalcy was abandoned.

In 1953 the same collection of buildings was re-renamed College of Southern Utah (CSU), implying that there was more to the school than just agriculture. There was great disappointment among alums who liked calling themselves "Aggies."

Sales of CSU sweatshirts and stationery remained steady until 1969 when the name changed again and everyone had to go out and buy stationery and clothing branded "SUSC" for Southern Utah State College. The new name implied that there were northern, eastern, and western colleges in Utah and further implied that there were some rogue schools in Utah not officially certified as "state" colleges. Without these implications the name would seem a trifle redundant, as it was just about the *only* college in that southern section of the state.

By 1991 BNS-BAC-CSU-SUSC was offering enough four-year degrees to earn the coveted "university" designation and so became Southern Utah University (SUU), although a more comprehensive name would be Southern Utah Branch Normal School of Agriculture University College.

It might have been less trouble if the pioneers had just agreed on a single-word name for the college. It seems to be working for Yale and Oxford, not to mention Cambridge and Harvard ("the SUU of the East").

1

Synchronicity, Utah

And see that all these things are done in wisdom and in order.
Word of Wisdom, Mosiah 4:27

The relentless sun slid down the horizon at last, letting the land breathe and be real again. In the desert outskirts of the little village, twilight shadows began to crawl like many-legged tarantulas among the manzanita and cholla cactus. An elder Mormon emerged and ventured to the edge of his porch. He sniffed the motionless air and cast a baleful eye upon the squat adobe building across the street, its door closed and windows shuttered against the prying eyes of the orthodox. He scrutinized the out-of-town license plates with disdain and disappeared back indoors.

It was a spring evening in 1965. The friends of the two Gentiles had gathered for a last supper. From the city of cedars they journeyed all the way south to the village named for the Virgin. (Not Mary, Utah: *Virgin*, Utah.) They had invited my wife and me in order to say good-bye, for we were soon to be among them no more.

It took place in a shuttered room that few Mormons had ever seen. Initiates gained access by means of a plain door behind a screen at the farthest end of the Bent Lizard Restaurant at 84000 S. 91500 W., Virgin, Utah. No signs betrayed its presence; no wide-flung door welcomed its patrons, for it was . . . a bottle club.

It was, as I said, 1965. Liquor laws prohibited the selling of drinks in public establishments. But if a person paid a membership fee to a bottle club, that person would gain access to a locker wherein to stash some hooch that he could retrieve to enjoy with his meal.

No one in the room that night knew the identities of the members of the Bent Lizard Bottle Club, the ones who had facilitated this farewell dinner. Or at least no one was supposed to know. What mattered was that bottles were brought out of locked lockers. Glasses of wine would be served with the Texas-size steaks or pork chops.

Sharon and I exchanged a little knowing glance when one of the guests told the waitress he would have the "park chop." The dialect of southern Utah, alien to us at first, had become a familiar reminder of where we were, sort of like visiting a foreign country where one is surrounded by exotic accents. In the speech of southern Utah we would use a fark to eat the cheesecake that came from the restaurant fredge. The farewell speeches following our mell would give us a tarrable nostalgia and maybe brang a tar to the eye, which would glisten in the candles' flickering yallow flame.

We had come to southern Utah as strangers and outlanders, and now we were being given a dinner complete with Gentile joy juice in our honor. More than this—and it took decades for me to fully appreciate it—there were several men in that room at the Bent Lizard who were to shape the next thirty years of my teaching career. Wes, who when asked would tell you he never had a bad day in his life. Next to him sat Harry, who labored in the face of great odds to teach me the difference between the terms "penultimate" and "quintessential." There was Gene, who showed me that laughter is not only the best medicine—

it's often the only inoculation against epidemics of ignorance. And Dick at the head of the table, who taught me enough about being a department chairman that I never wanted to be one. And of course there was Fred, who was proof that it was better to have a gleam in your eye than a shine on the seat of your pants.

I sipped my coffee and stared into the candle flame. What a coming-together these two years had been, what a web of coincidences, what a mélange of synchronicity. So many things had conspired to get us to that point and now we were about to pack up and leave Cedar City, Utah, the town where people who live in Parowan go for excitement.

Oh my heck.

Someone with an inclination toward philosophizing will doubtless find messages, meanings, and morals in my anecdotes. "Follow your bliss," "take what comes with good cheer," "stay open to new things," those kinds of clichés. However, if I were in the business of pushing bromides, this wouldn't be a book; it would be a needlepoint pillow or a bumper sticker.

Love was at the heart of the thing. I fell in love when I was a high school senior and Sharon was a sophomore. When I went off to college, Sharon loved me and so she followed. I finished the BA and I loved her, so I wanted to stick around while she piled up credits in microbiology. I therefore applied for graduate school. Being in school meant we could live cheap, for those were simple-living days, days when beans and hamburger made for a feast and a few cinder blocks and salvaged planks meant we could have a bookcase. All we really wanted was to keep doing what we both loved, namely going to classes, taking tests, writing papers, and necking. (See how one thing leads on to another? But more about our kids later.) However, as a writer named Bill Shakespeare wrote in *Hamlet*, there came a rub.

But not in the necking. The rub was personified in a teacher I rubbed the wrong way one too many times. He turned out to be our ticket to Utah.

Let's call him Rex Nostrom, which wasn't his real name. I won't use "Dr." because I'm not sure he had a doctorate and won't use "Professor" because I'm certain he never attained that illustrious title. He might have gotten as far as associate professor. Maybe. There's a ranking system in academia—instructors at the bottom, then assistant professors, then associate professors, and finally full professors at the top. The year I earned my own promotion into the top echelon I thought I might go over to the cemetery and pee on Nostrom's grave, but I figured the line would be too long.

Here's the story. At the time I began being an English major at Colorado State University (known as CSU, not to be confused with CSUtah)—notice my avoidance of the phrase "*studying* English"—the English department included drama, journalism, philosophy, and speech. I was looking around for a way to make a living with a degree in English, and journalism looked like the most logical answer. I had taken journalism in high school, been on the sports desk of the *Estes Park High School Mountaineer*, had done a few sports stories for the *Rocky Mountain News* and the *Estes Park Trail-Gazette*, and I'd written for the *CSU Collegian*. Thus it was that when Nostrom stood behind the podium of J-201: Reporting and told us in his pompous operatic voice that a good newspaper story must include the basics of What, Why, When, Where, and Who, I decided I'd look at the textbook to see if it was equally "basic." Sure enough, like his opening lecture, the textbook was aimed at an audience of fifteen-year-olds. In fact, it was the same book used in sophomore high school classes. I already knew the stuff, so I went to the registrar to drop the class.

The form asked "reason for dropping the class?" so I wrote down "it repeats a class I took in high school." Nostrum received his copy of the registrar's form and I, in turn, received his unalloyed, undisguised, unmerited, and enduring contempt.

Somewhere around that same time, this same Nostrum decided to display his baritone acting talents as King Creon in a reader's theater production of *Antigone*. The *Collegian* editor asked me to review the production, and I guess the term "over" appeared one too many times in my review, as in "overacting," "overrated," "overambitious," and "overly melodramatic."

In one of her cruel jests, Fate waved her magic wand and Rex Nostrum was turned into the chair of the Department of English. Other faculty in the department liked me, but Nostrum was powerful and most of them were afraid of him. As long as I didn't take any of his classes or make eye contact in the hallway, we got along OK. Until the day, that is, when I decided to apply for graduate school.

"Not while *I'm* chairman," he told me to my face. "You'll never get accepted into *my* department as a master's candidate."

But my father had taught me—mainly by example—that to a determined person there *is* no such thing as a "final authority" in such matters, and so I persevered until I *did* get accepted. I had had some outspoken advocates among the English faculty, three of whom were persons you would not want to get into a confrontation with. Nostrum may have been a bully toward students, but among authentic scholars he was an academic weenie.

After one quarter of graduate school I applied for a graduate teaching assistantship (GTA). Why? First of all, we needed money and it was easy work. Second, it would be a legitimate excuse to stretch the graduate work into two years, giving me time to figure out whatever my literary passion was supposed to be. Not that I cared all that much, but my graduate committee kept asking embarrassing questions about thesis topics and discipline concentrations, that sort of thing.

"Not in *this* department!" roared the Great Rex. "You'll never get a GTA here while *I'm* chairman!"

Up until that very moment I didn't really give a damn one way or the other. I could work for the newspaper part-time or even fall back on my other job, making weekend deliveries for Bowling's Fine Furniture. But when this puffed-up bag of wind told me I *couldn't* do it, I naturally had to. And I did. The very next quarter I was teaching two sections of E-2: Freshman Composition, and the following year I was selected by Dr. Claude Henry to be one of his personal teaching assistants in a new experimental class.

As for the chairman, he never forgave me. If you're ever in CSU's Morgan Library, look up my MA thesis, "W. E. Aytoun: Scottish Satirist," and have a glance at the committee signature page. Mine is probably the only thesis in that library in which the space for the chairman's signature is blank.

There is a needlepoint moral here, something along the lines of the Latin phrase about not letting the bastards grind you down. Or not quitting just because one person says you should. Or laughing in the face of doom. Something like that.

Spring 1963.

My fellow graduate teaching assistants and I spent final examination week and the following week grading stacks of freshman compositions and filling out grade reports. We shared a big room in the turn-of-the-century section of Old Main. The place was drafty, and it smelled from decades of floor wax and tobacco smoke. It had a high ceiling and tall, age-encrusted windows that let a little feeble sunshine fall on the eight army surplus desks, the conference table, and the metal stand where the coffeepot sat.

One by one the GTAs finished up their grade reports, dropped all the student essays into cardboard boxes in the hallway, cleaned out their desks, and left.

Me, I was late grading my papers because I'd been busy trying to get myself graduated. Thanks to a great stroke of synchronicity, our baby daughter, Stephanie, opted to enter our lives on the very day I was scheduled to take my graduate examination in French. The birth of Stephanie has always been a very special thing to me because I hadn't finished reading the one hundred required pages in *Histoire de Literature Francais*. The professor graciously gave me an extension.

It went like this: Love led to necking, necking led to baby Stephanie, and Stephanie's natal debut upon the Great Stage of Life precipitated a postponement of my French test, which not only saved my academic bacon but also resulted in me being the last one to be cleaning out my desk in the GTA room of Old Main when who should come clumping in but the clumping grump himself, Chairman Rex. He looked about the empty room vacantly (yes, that's a pun), and since I was invisible to him, he saw no one there.

"Anyone here?" he asked.

"*I'm* here," I said, truthfully. I noticed he was holding a flyer of some sort.

"Anyone else?"

"Nope. Looks like I'm the last one to finish up and get out of here."

I think he snorted, but I can't be sure. At any rate, he frowned his best King Creon frown and dropped the flyer on the coffee stand.

"You might as well have this then," he said.

It announced the availability of an out-of-state teaching job. No doubt Nostrom had received it in the mail and thought he would post it in the GTA office. But no one was left to read it, so in a few weeks he would have to take it down again, which would be an admission that it had been pointless to post it in the first place. He could toss it in the wastebasket, but that would seem irresponsible since some other chairman had entrusted it to him. Maybe he could send it back with a note saying that no one was interested, except that he didn't really know that. It was the kind of administrative decision, I suspect, that kept him awake nights.

The job opening was at the College of Southern Utah in a place bearing the pleasant-sounding name of Cedar City.

"Cedar City": I pictured a Tuscany postcard of a village with houses of whitewashed stone nestled beneath tall cedar trees, cheerful peasants singing as they carried water jugs from a little stream running alongside the cobbled street.

The job description mentioned teaching creative writing as well as freshman composition. My master's thesis was in Victorian poetry, but I had also taken every creative writing course the university offered, some of them twice.

Not only did the job seem like it would be worth looking into, but it just so happened that I'd be available. Our only commitment at the time was for summer jobs. Sharon was going back to her job at the Copper Penny Gift Shop in Estes Park, where she peddled Rocky Mountain souvenirs made in Japan to tourists from Germany. And I would return to my job in VIS and I/E with the U.S. Forest Service. ("Visitor Information Service" and "Information/Education" meant that I handed out brochures, cleaned outhouses, and answered tourist questions. In my spare time I fought forest fires.) But we had no prospects for the following autumn. I don't think we had really thought much about it. Maybe I'd look for a newspaper job. Like most young dreamers of the sixties, when we did discuss our future, it was mostly about whether we wanted to live in Denver or San Francisco or Florida and whether our little house would have a white picket fence or one made of wrought iron. (See the lyrics to the pop song "My Blue Heaven" as sung by Rudy Valee and you'll pretty much have the gist of our Philosophy of Life.)

Cedar City, Utah. Maybe, for a year? I would look into it.

Never in my life had I made a formal application for a job. I usually just walked in the door and asked. The only time I ever filled out papers was when I needed to get a Social Security card.

Not knowing how one went about applying, I figured the logical thing was to telephone the number provided on the College of Southern Utah flyer and ask for the job. If it was still open.

The call went straight through to Dick Rowley, chairman of English. Innocent as I was, it did not strike me as odd that it hadn't gone through at least two secretaries. Anyway, he asked me about myself and I told him. Yes, I could probably teach journalism. Creative writing? Heck, I'd been in every creative writing class offered at CSU. Photography? I admitted I was a little weak there, but assured him I knew my way around a camera, mostly an Argus C3.

Married? Yup. With two adorable little girls. There was Caprise, who came along shortly after my bachelor's degree, and Stephanie, whose birth came in time to postpone my MA language exam. Son Robert would have to wait until I needed a PhD.

Religion? Presbyterian. Sort of semi-regular on attendance, though.

"You sound like the person we're looking for," he said. "Can you send me your credentials?"

And here's the *really* dumb part. I did not have a clue what he meant by "credentials."

"Well, a list of courses you've taught. A grade transcript. Your degrees. Your publications. Oh, and letters of reference."

"Reference?"

"Maybe a letter from your chairman?"

"Maybe not," I said. "I think he's on vacation or something. How about if I get a couple of my professors to write to you?"

"Fine."

Professors Robert Zoellner, Claude Henry, and Les Stimmel were more than glad to write glowing accounts of my creative teaching, my concern for detail, my professionalism. Then again, they would say just about anything about me if it would get up Rex Nostrum's nose.

I mailed off my "credentials" and cleaned out my desk. Sharon and I moved our few pieces of furniture to a cozy rental cabin in Estes Park the following week. Our plan was to hike and fish and generally mess around while waiting to begin our summer jobs. We had just started the messing around part, however, when the phone rang. The English department chairman at Cedar City would like to interview me.

Since we had a few days to spare, the timing was perfect. Dad agreed to loan us his almost-new Olds Cutlass. Mom said that he also agreed to take care of Caprise and Stephanie for us while we were gone.

I was the proud bearer of a squeaky-new master of arts degree but didn't know from applications and had no clue what "credentials" meant. It would soon become obvious that I also didn't know what "Mormon" referred to, nor did I know jack about the Church of Jesus Christ of Latter-day Saints. All I knew was that we had made the drive to Cedar City, and I was standing in Chairman Rowley's office where he was offering me $5,400 for nine months. And I'd be in charge of all writing programs above the freshman level. Holy cow! I mean, oh my heck!

In specific terms this meant that I was going to teach basic journalism, photography, creative writing (drama, fiction, poetry), advanced essay, and feature article writing. I would also teach freshman composition and a civic extension course in vocabulary building. Me. I mean, *me*? I stood there staring at Chairman Rowley. I was studying his face to see whether he was kidding. (Living with my dad had gotten me into a habit of doing that.)

"Looking to see if I have horns?" he said, smiling.

"Huh?" I replied intelligently.

"No horns, no tail. And I don't have a sacramental undershirt with holes in it either."

Now I understood the situation. I was conversing with a lunatic.

"See you in September," he said, laughing, and handed me a check to cover our mileage and travel expenses.

I was green. Except for NRA marksmanship I had never taught anything except freshman composition, I had a pretty wife and two little girls, and I couldn't have obtained a recommendation from my chairman if I put a gun to his head. And all of a sudden here I was, a full-time instructor in charge of creative writing at a real college. A college, I should add, that was just changing from being a two-year institution to being a four-year one. This meant there would be pressure, but I didn't care. Bring it on.

After leaving Rowley's office I walked around to see the campus. I was greeted by several faculty. I had the feeling they had come to look at me like neighbors coming to see the new puppy. We chatted but I didn't learn much about the College of Southern Utah except that I would be answerable to two terrifying powers: the Church at Salt Lake City and the university board at Logan.

"Guess we got a job," I told Sharon when I got back to the King's Rest Motel. "If you want to live here."

"Why not?" she said. "Do you want to neck before we go to lunch?"

We necked, had lunch, and the next day drove home to Colorado to tell friends and relations that we'd be moving to Utah at the end of summer.

So . . . love led to grad school, dropping a class led to animosity, a baby's birth led to a delayed French test, and naïveté led to southern Utah. Someday I would find out why I was really there, just as someday I would discover what valuable friends I had in the three faculty members back in Colorado. Meanwhile,

I had a few things to do, such as learning how to teach journalism and photography and finding out whether there was a Presbyterian church in Cedar City. Little did I know that within two years I was also going to learn to be a religious diplomat and black market bourbon runner.

2

Academic Affairs

Wherefore, he that preacheth and he that receiveth, understand one another, and both are edified and rejoice together.

Doctrine and Covenants 50:22

With an orange U-Haul trailer clamped to the bumper of our green Nash Ambassador station wagon, we chugged over the mountain passes and along the rivers and puttered down through the cedar-fringed valleys of southern Utah until we came at last to the quiet little town of Cedar City, where we would rent a place and get settled in.

During our college years Sharon and I had become pretty blasé about finding rental apartments. Usually we'd show up a week before class, check the local newspaper ads, inspect two or three apartments, and take one of them. The idea of a rental shortage never occurred to us. However, after a week of living in the King's Rest Motel while watching the newspaper and checking the Laundromat bulletin board for rentals, we were forced to accept the fact that in the vast metropolis of Cedar City only one house was for rent.

We rented it, but how to describe it?

I could begin with the sand. The yard was sand, the driveway was sand, and when the wind blew from the direction of

St. George, Utah, the windowsills and linoleum were also sand. Fine red sand. A couple of thirsting elm trees stood dejectedly in the front sand; the back sand had been landscaped by a pile of old lumber artfully arranged to look like disused boards complete with weeds and cactus and actual wasp and ant nests. Very authentic—Early Southern Utah Semi-Abandoned.

The house itself had begun life either as a mobile home or as some prototype version of a modular unit. The modular/mobile part included bedrooms at each end and a bathroom in the middle. During the second stage of the house's existence, the owner had dug a cellar in which to keep a collection of local mold spores and spiders; on top of the cellar he built a living room and kitchen. The windows were a little loose; even when they were closed and locked, the slightest breeze would still lift the curtains and coat the windowsill with red silt. The gap where the mobile home part joined the addition was wide enough to pass notes through. Or a small cat. The place was either freezing cold or roasting hot, depending on the outside temperature and angle of the sun.

From this domicile I sallied forth each day to do battle with the forces of ignorance, bringing what I had been told would be a whole new program of creative writing to a backward college in the provinces. There was one weird coincidence. Both Colorado State and Southern Utah were called CSU. At both schools I worked in a building named Old Main that sat near a street named College Avenue. Appropriately for a teacher who was to make an invaluable contribution to Utah knowledge, I was given a big office with an adjoining conference room in case I should want to conduct seminars. Or take a nap on the conference table. The department had a secretary to type my class handouts and order my textbooks for me. It was even hinted that I might (don't tell anyone) sometimes get away with smoking my pipe in my office, so long as I kept the door shut and the windows wide open. Chairman Rowley trusted me so much that he put me in charge of office management.

"Office management" meant that I was expected to keep track of the paper and pencils and mimeograph fluid. Mimeo fluid came in one-gallon cans and was mostly alcohol. A faculty member said it seemed appropriate to entrust the alcohol to the department's only Gentile, but I wasn't sure what he meant.

Things could not have been more promising for a kid who was just starting out in teaching. The only drawback to my new academic estate was my desk, a tiny one-pedestal thing of the sort sometimes referred to as a "student" or "stenographer" desk.

At the College of Southern Utah I found myself involved in several plots and schemes, most of them harmless. There was, for example, the time when the department chairman became alarmed at the amount of paper being used to reproduce class handouts. The department boasted both a hand-cranked ditto machine (purple ink, messy, temperamental) and an electric mimeograph machine (black ink, even more messy and temperamental), either of which could mutilate fifty sheets of paper in the blink of an eye.

The chairman's response to the shocking waste of ditto and mimeo paper was decisive and quick. He ordered me to take the entire paper supply to my office and lock it up. Only he and I would have keys to the paper cupboard, and I would dole it out to the faculty sheet by sheet after first determining that each handout was important and necessary. I became the ream czar. But the rate of depletion continued unabated. The chairman himself, it turned out, was the culprit. He dashed off examples, instructions, charts, and memos to his students whenever the urge struck him.

Being the new guy, I wasn't about to confront him. Instead, I entered into a conspiracy with the other five members of the English department. I issued each of them enough reams of paper to get through the semester, which they hid in their own offices. Then whenever the chairman told me he was taking "a few sheets" to make a handout, I pointed out that the supply was running low and he might reconsider the need for the freshmen to have a typed copy of the latest *Newsweek* article against logging virgin forests.

Another conspiracy involved the college PR man named Brad, an athletic young fellow. He bounced into my office one day announcing that he did the photography and public relations work for the college and sometimes taught journalism, and had the chairman given me the keys to the photo lab yet?

Photo lab? What photo lab?

He helped me search the desk and credenza for the keys, which is when another odd thing took place. On a shelf in the credenza we found a few dozen two-year-old LDS church bulletins that had apparently been reproduced on the department's mimeograph machine. My new acquaintance grabbed them up and stuffed them into his briefcase. There was no other form of Mormon material in that whole room. Had there been some illegal reproduction going on in my office? Or was there some kind of secret information in those church bulletins, something I was not allowed to see? It was almost as though he feared that I would be tainted if I handled them. Kind of like my mother used to say about certain magazines.

"Tell you what," my visitor said in a confiding undertone. "I can help you teach photography. Know how to develop film?"

"Nope."

"Tell you what, then. I'll teach you to develop and print pictures, and you give me one of the darkrooms to use. And I'll want to use the enlargers too."

So here was another mystery. I had explored most of the campus, which consisted of eight or nine buildings (depending on whether you counted the bomb shelter where the groundskeeper kept his machines) plus a gymnasium, and nowhere had I seen anything indicating a photo lab, let alone darkrooms (plural) and (plural) photo enlargers.

Brad led me out of the office, out of Old Main, and up the stairs of an adjoining building. Up and up until we got to the third or fourth floor. He took my keys and opened a door.

"Here you go," he said. "We had a teacher here who was nuts about photography. He had the school build this. Well, his father and his uncle are both bishops, if you know what I mean."

Not a clue what he meant. How could knowing a bishop in the Church of Jesus Christ of Latter-day Saints help someone get a darkroom?

The photo lab consisted of six small darkrooms for students to use, a faculty darkroom, two big enlargers, and an even bigger apparatus called a "floor enlarger."

"Suppose you took a picture of your wife," Brad said. "With this baby you could make a print big enough to cover your whole wall."

Could help with the drafts coming through our house.

I learned that "we" had a cupboard full of cameras, mostly of the reflex variety. Several Yashicas, a Leica or two, numerous Argus Reflexes. Another cupboard contained 35 mm black-and-white film in bulk, which we could wind into film canisters in our darkroom. Chemicals by the gallon. Photo paper by the pound. Brad taught me the use of it all, and he even volunteered to teach the class in photo developing so I wouldn't have to. All he wanted in return was the private use of one of the darkrooms.

I never saw any of the pictures Brad developed in the late night hours up there, and a tiny voice in my head told me I didn't want to.

I was beginning to suspect that my chief asset was naïveté. If I kept quiet and went on looking like I had a lot to learn, I might manage to keep my job for another year.

Long-term employment didn't really cross my mind at that point in my life. I never set out to become the World's Greatest Literature Professor. I saw the Cedar City job as a way to pass the time while waiting for a newspaper job to open up. I was also waiting for a letter from the Case Tractor Company in

Chicago, telling me they loved my advertising ideas and would hire me to write ads and instruction manuals. My best slogan, in my mind, was "Depend on Case: we back our tractors—but we don't stand behind our manure spreaders." Why Case Tractors never answered my letter is a mystery to this day.

As Brad went on talking about teaching photography I realized that I knew even less about how to do that than I did about developing film. Fortunately, he had a couple of days in which to show me how to use the darkrooms, and I had a copy of the photography textbook. With any luck I could stay a chapter ahead of the students.

I wasn't much worried about it. In every summer job I had ever had—tour bus driver, sporting goods salesman, fire fighter—I found out that I was OK once I had figured out my situation and adjusted my thinking to it.

Some people never seemed to make the adjustment, though.

We met an advertising man in Cedar City, for instance, a wheeler-dealer who owned more three-piece suits than I owned Jockey shorts (six) and never tired of talking about the multimillion-dollar ad programs he was designing for the local family-owned pharmacy. He planned on making millions by writing ads for the car dealership where they sold ten new Fords per year and knew two years ahead of time who was going to buy them. This ad expert was thoroughly frustrated and thoroughly miserable in Cedar City.

Back in Colorado I had known an equally frustrated forest ranger. This guy had attended college for four years and joined the U.S. Forest Service, dreaming of the day when he could drive a jeep into the deep woods and hobnob with hobnailed loggers while watching big muscled chaps in checkered shirts cut down enormous trees. The roar of the chainsaws, the whoosh of the tree coming down, the massive trucks loading up with their diesels roaring. But he was in the Estes Park district of the Roosevelt National Forest, a district that is mainly a recreation area without any logging. His official pickup truck didn't even have four-wheel drive. His job consisted mainly of doing the toilet paper inventory for the campgrounds and answering the same tourist questions over and over and over and over.

When I worked for the forest service, I had no lofty image of myself. I was totally happy in my role of unspecialized government worker. When a lady asked me how to deal with the dwarf mistletoe infecting her decorative spruce, I (English major, remember) simply said "eliminate the host" and she was happy. I managed to get all the way off of her property before she realized I had told her to cut down her favorite tree.

Up in the CSUtah darkroom, an older guy from class asked me how to improve his photographic portrait of his wife.

"I could suggest some professional techniques," I said, "but I think it would be better for you to do some experimenting with this enlarger gadget and these filter thingies and figure them out for yourself. You'll learn a lot more than if I just tell you."

The first real literary intellectual I met while careering along in my undergraduate career at Colorado State University was Bob Zoellner, the youngest PhD ever to grace the alma mater's English faculty. Graduate students feared him; older faculty distrusted him. Zoellner would not only give you an F on an essay that had cost you three weeks of entombment in the library, he would yell in your face that you were a hopeless moron if you asked why.

"But," you would argue, "I spent three weeks writing that paper!"

"If you spent three weeks and this is all you could come up with," he'd say, "you really need to consider some major other than English."

Colorado State was still a land-grant university in those days. Small and lonely in a climate of agriculture and engineering, the English department was a hotbed of dusty literature and banal discussions. To counteract the dulling effect and preserve his sanity, Zoellner assembled a circle of eccentrics, sort of a defensive square like nineteenth-century infantry formed whenever they were attacked by cavalry. He found people he could talk with and made them "his people." He invited them to his house to drink Manhattans and say rude things about e. e. cummings. One of his people was a junkyard owner with an MA in literature who loved to talk Spenser and Swift while haggling over the value of a snarl of copper wire or a worn-out car battery. There was me, the hillbilly kid who asked lots of questions and would let him use my apartment on weekends. I also took him deer hunting. The Zoellner Irregulars also included an assistant professor in physics. This guy not only knew when the world would end but was pretty certain he would have a hand in it. And don't let's forget our favorite firebrand among local intellects, Father Malcolm Boyd, the Episcopalian chaplain who published *Are You Running With Me, Jesus?* He held all-night rap sessions in his basement, which in hippie fashion was painted black and furnished with floor cushions and old mattresses.

But let's get back to Cedar City.

Soon after my arrival I was visited by a mysterious character whom I'm going to call Rabbi Weinstein. And the mystery was, what in the name of the Talmud was he doing in Cedar City? At the time I met him, I didn't know enough about Jews and Mormons to even ask the question.

Anyhow, one fine autumn day I was in my oversized office trying to figure out which papers to keep in my undersized desk and which to forever entomb in the credenza. There was a soft knocking on the doorframe and into the room stepped a small man in black clothing, wearing a little black yarmulke on the back of his skull.

He admired the view from my windows, complimented me on the table and matching chairs in my conference room, read several titles among the books on my shelves, and asked me if I smoked. Or drank coffee.

"I smoke a pipe," I admitted. "And I don't seem to function well unless I've had a couple of cups of coffee."

"Thank God," he said. "Now we are six."

"Six?"

"Six for coffee breaks. Twice a week, sometimes three times. I'll bring you the schedule. Our little clique includes myself, a Catholic from biology, one fallen-away Mormon, another man who is 'Church' but likes his coffee and Scotch, and one very devout atheist. Each week, twice a week, we meet. On the highway at the edge of town there is a truck stop where we drink coffee and smoke. Can you drive?"

"We have a station wagon."

Why did I feel like a POW helping plan an escape from Stalag Fünfzehn?

"Good. I will tell the others. And I will bring you a schedule," he said. As the rabbi took his leave, he turned back with one more question.

"Professor Work, I understand you are a Presbyterian?"

"That's right."

"Let me welcome you to the ghetto."

And with that I met my first Jewish Gentile.

Learning about the CCK—Clandestine Coffee Klatch—helped explain a puzzle that I'd come across in my explorations of the campus. You know how students always shun sidewalks and wear crooked paths across the grass? At CSUtah I noticed bare dirt tracks leading from the four main classroom buildings out to the streets at the edge of campus. But there were no bus stops, no street crossings, no particular reason for a well-beaten trail to go there. These worn paths in the grass did not lead from building to building, only to the edge of the campus.

Like caffeinated beverages, tobacco in any form was prohibited on campus. The entire place, indoors and outdoors, was a no-smoking zone. I had a suspicion that the physical education department had created this ingenious setup. Any students who chose to smoke were required to perform a 100-yard dash to the edge of campus, have their cigarette, then run back before the ten-minute class break was over. Maybe the exercise offset the lung damage.

The Student Union had vending machines for lemon-lime sodas, but you could not get any kind of caffeine on campus. The only place to buy Coke or Dr Pepper or a cup of java was at some café or the truck stop on the edge of town that catered to "outsiders." After having spent six years socializing in the smoke haze of the CSU Student Union basement drinking bottomless mugs of Guatemala's second-worst export, I found it strange to walk into the CSUtah Student Union where the air was clean and the strongest drink on offer was an orange-flavored concoction perpetually churning away in a big plastic dispenser on the counter. Students either had to carry their own caffeine or do without.

Funny thing was, they seemed just as alert and intelligent as the ones back home.

I think I met the dancer during the first year in Utah but I can't be certain. I do remember her last name, but it wouldn't be a good idea to publish it.

CSUtah could not have cared less whether a faculty member did research and wrote juried articles. But the administration did lay heavy emphasis upon community service. You know, like when you're arrested for driving 60 mph through a liquor store (especially if it doesn't have a drive-up) and you have to pick up garbage along the highway for the next ten years?

Some faculty opted to be assistant scout leaders. But Boy Scout groups were all associated with churches, which meant Mormon. There was a Presbyterian church, but it had only three male Gentiles of scouting age.

The other option was to offer service courses such as vocabulary building, business math, income tax preparation, and so forth. These usually met in the evening, as long as it was an evening that was not scheduled for Church functions such as Family Night, Men's Night, Women's Night, Service Night, or Basketball Night . . . in other words, service classes met Wednesday evening.

My service course, I was told, would be creative writing: nonfiction. The clientele consisted of wannabe writers from the community, most of whom wanted to write about their ancestors who were Mormon pioneers. I learned that many of them had been taking the course for years, perpetually revising the same manuscript. One old lady had a thick sheaf of paper that told how her ancestors had pushed and pulled a handcart all the way through Nebraska and over the Rocky Mountains to Utah. She insisted that I use a #2 pencil to make comments in the margin of her story; I discovered by accident that when she got home she carefully erased all my corrections.

Another of the after-hours students was an obnoxious woman who had lost feminine attractiveness shortly after WWII but fancied herself quite the flirt. She dyed her hair red, wore tight clothing, and delighted in teasing young male instructors. No one else in class seemed to like her. Whereas the other students were polite to me and made generous allowances for my youth and inexperience, she seemed bent upon making me blush and stammer.

But one evening I learned how old punch lines can still have value. I also learned not to hold back when it comes to dealing with class disturbances.

I was taking the roll when my tormentor remarked that she had seen me with my family at the grocery store.

"Your wife is certainly attractive!" she gushed, her voice dripping with implication.

"Thank you," I said, thinking I would now get on with the lesson.

"And your little daughters!" she continued. "The older one is *very* blonde!"

At this point she was addressing the entire classroom.

"She is *so* blonde!"

And then she came to her point.

"But you and your wife, of course, you're both brunette. I mean, I couldn't help but wonder why your little girl would be so *blonde*!"

Somewhat dumbfounded, I fell back on an old cliché.

"It must have been the milkman," I said with a smile.

Dead silence fell on the classroom. Then came a low rumble of barely suppressed giggling. My nemesis blushed beet-red and clamped her mouth shut. And so far as I can recall, she never spoke in class again. Our milkman, it turned out, was her husband.

However, I digress: I was going to talk about Mrs. Marty Kean.

Up until that time I had only taught as a GTA, and my only "office" was a desk in a room shared by all the GTAs. Carrying a full load of graduate classes, I had virtually no time at all to talk with my students on a one-to-one basis. I used to tell them to say their name to me if they ever ran into me outside of class or else I wouldn't remember them. "I never remember names," I often said, "but I *do* forget faces."

There were, of course, many stories about luscious female students who traded heavy necking and surreptitious sex acts for grades. One Colorado State University legend concerned "Thunderbird Sally," who drove around in a two-seater, powder-blue convertible and seduced professors until it was discovered that she had never actually enrolled at the university. Another was the buxom gal whose grade average was in trouble, so she propositioned all her teachers in order to bring those grades up. Despite her extracurricular efforts she flunked English, math, chemistry, world history, and physical education anyway, but she received an A in P-142: Ethics.

Mrs. Marty Kean either taught dancing or was assisting the teacher. The thing was, at least according to *her*, she had to dash from her dancing class at the gymnasium straight to my class in creative writing. She would sit there in the front row all flushed and glowing from her "dash," wearing a trench coat that gaped open enough to show a nice pair of legs encased in black tights.

One night after class she followed me back to my office on some pretext or other. The only part I recall is the moment she shed her trench coat and stood there in the glow of my desk lamp wearing tight black tights and a tight black leotard. Her dancing outfit, she apologized. It's why she never took off the coat in class.

In short order, during which time she came closer and closer to me until I was literally pinned against my desk—and the desk was sliding along the floor toward the wall—I learned that her husband was in the military and was stationed in Germany, that she was very lonely especially at night, that most of the women in town didn't want to socialize with her (oh, really? Gee, imagine that!), and that she and her husband had been married at the temple in Salt Lake City. Maybe she used some other word for her temple marriage, something involving seals, which conjured up a mental image of something black, sleek, and wet. Which was a thought I did not need at that particular juncture. Anyway, I recall her saying "temple."

Thank God for religion, that's what I say.

I pried her fingers off my lapels and remarked that she had pronounced "The Temple" as if the words were capitalized.

"At Salt Lake City," she said. "You know, the temple?"

Not a clue, thank you very much. I had heard about the Temple of Solomon somewhere, and back in Fort Collins there was a Masonic temple. Why a temple in Salt Lake City would be special I had no idea.

She took my hands and placed them on her hips.

"So, tell me about this temple place," I suggested, climbing onto the desk in a semi-fetal crouch.

I'm still not too clear on the actual rules and regulations involved, but I later learned that when a couple goes to Salt Lake City to take their vows at the temple itself, there is some kind of superpowerful bonding that takes place. If she and hubby had only been joined by a justice of the peace in back of a gas station in Hebing or in a neighborhood church in Dry Wash, she would be OK with shedding her leotard and conjoining with me right there on the floor next to my wire wastebasket. Unfortunately, theirs had been a temple wedding and, "Well, you know what *that* means!"

"So is it like a regular wedding?" I asked, wiping my sweaty palms on my pants and dropping into my swivel chair. "Except for the venue, I mean?"

Slowly, gradually, I got her to describe the wedding, then her hubby, then her home back in wherever-it-was. After a while she put the coat back on and went on talking about wards and bishops and the difference between the temple and the tabernacle. I learned that a ward was kind of like a congregation of church members within a certain area of town. A bishop is in charge of a ward, like a pastor. It seems that some places have so many bishops you can't throw a rock without hitting one. Several people have tried.

Mrs. Kean even shared the story of the great locust plague with me and told me how God sent seagulls to eat the locusts and that's why there's a statue of a seagull on top of that pillar in Salt Lake City. For some reason I thought it was a duck.

There's a lesson for young teachers here. Whenever you are teaching a night class and a sexy babe in a leotard makes a pass at you after hours, get her to talk about religion. It's a sure way to prevent getting overexcited. Theology seems to be a kind of birth control.

As my generation got older and older and began to approach "transitional retirement" like a herd of decrepit bison being shoved over the cliff, I found myself attending more and more retirement functions. On one such occasion I thought it would be nice of me to acknowledge what the retiring honoree had taught me.

"You know, Joanne," I said, "years ago you told me how you ended a tedious office visit by standing and gently leading the person out the door and down the hall, as if you were going to walk with them to their car. I want to thank you for that. I've used the trick more times than I could count."

"Really?" Joanne said, absentmindedly dipping her cheese cube in her cheap white wine. "I don't remember telling you about that."

Likewise, several teachers at CSUtah had a long and lasting influence on my teaching, an influence they would probably not recall. Or not admit to.

Professor Harry Plummer, for example, taught vocabulary building and was my mentor in teaching the community outreach version of the class. Harry reset my mental machinery. Even though I'd had all those creative writing classes, I had never given much thought to word choices and certainly not to word origins. I liked words well enough, but after knowing him I could never again pass up a new word without looking into it. Here was a man who seemed to know every word in the English language and all of their origins. He used words the way a painter uses a palette. Borrow a pencil from him or ask him how his weekend went, and you were in for a dazzling display of linguistic erudition. Wonderfully voluble without an iota of verbosity, etymologically erudite while eschewing circumlocution, he could also be a model of taciturnity, not to mention obmutescence. I wanted to be like him. I could never hope to match his mastery of vocabulary, but as a model of decorum and a zealot concerning language he has stayed with me all these years.

As has Eugene Woolf, who was possibly the best-loved professor at CSUtah. Being alphabetically adjacent, we sat next to one another on registration day, pencils poised to sign up students for our classes. I saw thirty students queued up in the hope of getting into one of Woolf's classes in American literature. Some teachers would sit at their tables all day long, looking as lonely as insurance salesmen at a church social. Among Gene's secrets of professorial success was a single word: fun. "The semester when teaching stops being fun for me," he would say, "is the semester I stop teaching."

He never put negative comments on student papers. He liked the game of finding something positive to say, even if it was only "nice margins!" or "here you used a word exactly right!" He hated teaching anything the same way twice, loved to discover some new angle, some recent scholarly article that would challenge what he thought about a piece.

One time I tried to help him. He was teaching Hawthorne's *The Scarlet Letter* and was looking for something new to say about it.

"Hey!" I offered. "I read recently that scholars have discovered what the 'A' on Hester Prynne's dress stood for!"

"What?"

"Abalone!"

"Why?"

"You know . . . mother of pearl? Ha, ha, ha!"

Apparently Gene's rule against negative criticism did not extend into humorous discourse between friends.

Somehow somebody came up with the idea of having Eugene Woolf and James Work team up on students in a class in American literature. That's how I found out the secret to his popularity. Humor. As a lecturer, Gene made Johnny Carson look like a rank amateur. I know this is true because after hearing Gene deliver a lecture on Melville I went home and watched Johnny Carson on the television.

"Amateur," I said, sneering at the TV screen.

So, I said to myself, it's possible, even permissible, to use stand-up comedy while teaching literary works about evil, murder, rape, debauchery, war, disease, and plague! Even *Moby Dick* can be funny, if you go at it the right way. The only time Gene did not punctuate a lecture with humor was while we were teaching Mark Twain, which made Twain seem even funnier than usual. Try it yourself: read "The Celebrated Jumping Frog of Calaveras County" with a completely deadpan face and your audience will soon be in convulsions. But don't think for a moment that Gene sacrificed serious literature for amusement: he taught literature brilliantly. It's just that he had discovered how to keep students awake and interested by holding out to them the possibility of some improvisational comedy.

A decade or two afterward, when I was being considered for promotion to associate professor, some faculty evaluator summed up my classroom performance with a phrase that included the words "stand-up comic." Gene would have been *so* proud of me!

If it ain't fun no more, don't do it no more.

Let me tell you a story about an opposite example, a man who did not find anything amusing about literature. Chaucer, to be exact.

Three things went into making our house in Cedar City the scene of several cocktail parties. First among these was the finished basement. I'll explain later how we moved from the bimodular nonmobile home house into a two-story brick; let it suffice for now to say that the move gave us a basement. A basement into which the neighbors couldn't see. Back in those days it was popular to turn such places into recreation rooms. They would staple acoustical tile to the ceiling, nail imitation wood paneling to the walls, put asphalt tile on the floor (including a shuffleboard design), and furnish it with a scattering of Naugahyde couches and chairs.

In addition to having our hideaway recreation room, we belonged to a church that was not officially averse to the consumption of alcohol. Third, I had an official Utah Liquor Authority Customer Identification card (you needed a state-issued ID card to purchase liquor). On any given weekend, therefore, you might find us with our friends in the dark of our personal catacombs, speaking in tongues and drawing occult symbols in the wet rings left on the coffee table by sweating beer bottles.

Let's name him George Walsh. Not his real name. Not even his real initials. He was the CSUtah expert in some dry and arcane subject such as sociology or perhaps mathematics. He drank once in a while and the Church knew it, but he was a straight arrow otherwise and an effective teacher, so it was overlooked.

On the evening in question, the Works were having a "cocktail party." (They were called that even though we never served anything fancy enough to be called a cocktail. Drinks of choice included vodka screwdrivers, bourbon with 7UP, and tiny cans of malt liquor.) As in Robert Burns's poem about Tam O'Shanter, the heavier the drinking became, the more amusing everyone seemed to get. There being a few English teachers among this group of cheery sots, the name Chaucer inevitably popped up.

"Chaucer!" burbled George the straight arrow. "Chaucer? Hell, I know that damn Chaucer!"

Before anyone could prevent it, George ascended the coffee table. Standing there with his head nearly touching the acoustic tiles and his torso swaying under the dual influence of Country Club Malt Liquor and gravity, he began to declaim the prologue from *The Canterbury Tales*:

Whan that Aprill with his shoures soote
The droghte of March hath perced to the roote,
And bathed every veyne in swich licour
Of which vertu engendred is the flour . . .

"Hold it!" I said, running to grab my Cambridge edition of *The Works of Geoffrey Chaucer*. I flew back to the party with it. (Flying Chaucers.)

"I'm ready now. Do it again!" I said.

He did do it again and nearly got it letter-perfect, 162 lines of the prologue in Middle English. There were about seven hundred lines left to go, but he had made his point. And this from a guy who wore a plastic pocket protector and thought Robert Frost was probably a fairy, that all of Shakespeare's works were written by someone else with the same name, and that all Emily Dickinson needed was a good romp in the hay with the gardener. After all, that's what brought Lady Chatterley around.

Some days after that he and I were cutting firewood and I asked him about his amazing recitation.

"High school," he said. "High school English teacher caught me talking in class while he was teaching Chaucer. For punishment I had to memorize the prologue. I hated that queer."

"Chaucer?"

"Him too."

So there I was, barely into my first year as a literature instructor, being befriended by one man who had suffered literature as punishment and another who saw it as mental entertainment. Which of these teaching philosophies, I wondered, would be mine?

Well, duh.

3

Are Assistant Professors Smart Enough to Shovel Gravel?

Be of good cheer, for I will lead you along.
Doctrine and Covenants 78:18

Those who can, do: those who can't, teach. Those who can do neither are called administrators.
Attributed to George Bernard Shaw

I was a dean, but now I'm clean.
M. F. Heiser

How many administrators does it take to change a light bulb? Well, before answering, we need to form a committee and look into how other universities change their light bulbs.

I'm not given to flat statements.

I will, however, make one concerning the cartload of administrators I have known: only two ever stood out as being the sort of boss I would gladly work for forever. And I see no point in trying to disguise the name of the first one, because anyone who went to CSUtah or taught there during his reign will recognize him from the following anecdotes. I refer to Dr. Royden Braithwaite, director of the College of Southern Utah. I even liked his title: "presidents" preside, mostly from a distance and buffered by a squadron of vice presidents who make the actual (and occasional) physical contact with faculty. Dr. Braithwaite directed. He directed his troops from the front line and he did it up close and personal.

Unknown to Chairman Rowley (not to mention the rest of the faculty), Dr. Braithwaite and I formed a firm alliance early in my CSUtah career. I had published two poems and three newspaper articles by that time, so he dubbed me the "poet and creative writer" of his campus.

I lectured for thirty years after leaving Utah and the only time an administrator ever visited my classroom was when an English chairman at Colorado State showed up in hopes of finding a reason not to promote me. Chairs, deans, and vice presidents ignored my periodic invitations to drop in: new chairpersons, replacement deans—not one of them took me up on it. Their job was to keep the stream of paperwork flowing in and out of the office, not to interact with faculty.

Dr. Braithwaite liked to stroll his campus. It was common to see him inspecting a sidewalk, talking to a tree, slapping some student on the back, or peering into a classroom just to see what was going on. He loved his campus. One day as I was teaching freshman composition I saw him walk past the open door. And heard his footsteps stop. Next thing I knew, he had slipped in and was leaning against the back wall, watching me at work.

He left before class was over. Some days later, though, he stopped in my office. And now it's time for an informational digression: in all my years of teaching I never learned how to schedule my time in order to have a set of papers graded before the next set was handed in.

Dr. Braithwaite therefore found me in the conference room arranging stacks of student essays on the conference table. (Arranging student essays first by alphabet, then by topic, then by grade average, then according to the first letter of the second paragraph is a great way to put off grading them.)

"Files?" he asked. I think he thought I was sorting through my poems to find one or two to publish.

"No, sir. This is a stack of sixty freshman themes I need to grade before Friday. That stack next to it is thirty literature essay tests I finished last night. This pile over here came from the evening nonfiction class, but I don't need to finish them until Wednesday next."

"Hmm," said The Director.

That same afternoon a secretary came from the director's office, pushing a furniture dolly with a big cardboard box on it.

"Director Braithwaite would like to borrow your stacks of student papers," she said. "Just over the weekend. I'll return them first thing Monday morning, if that's all right."

When she brought them back, she told me that his visual aid had been a great success at the meeting of the college's governing board. He stacked my papers in a foot-high pile and said to the board, "This is just *one* week's paperwork for *one* instructor! We need money for more people!"

His was a kind of logic with which there was no arguing.

When he dropped in to thank me for the loan of the papers, he suddenly became very quiet, looking at my very small desk, the one that was more or less the size of an end table.

"There's nothing on your desk," he observed. "I've never seen such an orderly desk."

He was right. All my junk and clutter was piled on the conference table. My desktop accoutrements consisted of my college-issued nameplate, my telephone, and a pencil holder that had begun life as a container for orange juice concentrate.

"That's because it's so small," I said. "There's no place for a mess. If I want to have any room on it, I have to keep it cleaned off. There's no place to shove things aside. I have to deal with anything as soon as it comes in."

"So it's too *small* to be cluttered," he said. "I like that."

In a few days, two men from the physical plant showed up in my office. Without much ceremony they emptied my two desk drawers, put the phone on the floor, and took away my little desk. They returned with Dr. Braithwaite's executive-size slab of walnut with two file cabinet pedestals. The top was the size of a regulation Ping-Pong table. If I was sitting behind it and wanted something lying on either end, I had to stand up and walk around to get it.

"Dr. Braithwaite wants you to have his desk. He's taking yours," the man from physical plant explained. "He says he was tired of seeing his cluttered up all the time, and you told him the secret."

And until I left Utah, I rarely saw the wood of that monster desk. The desktop grew into a mountain of ungraded papers, unopened mail, ignored flyers, and discarded lunch sacks. With the United States and the Soviet Union brandishing atomic intercontinental ballistic missiles at one another, school kids were being drilled on how to "duck and cover" under their desks. If there was a total nuclear holocaust I could rest easy, knowing if Moscow missed Alamogordo or Los Alamos and clobbered Cedar City instead, I'd be safe underneath that desk and its load of undone paperwork.

Now we come to the Harbrace affair. I'm hoping that its victims are long since retired and no longer interested in forming a lynch mob to hang the instructor responsible.

It was me.

Dr. Braithwaite walked into my office one day and put a letter down on the pile of rubble and refuse covering his former desk. He waited while I read it. It was from a CSUtah alum, he told me. In one single page, the writer had managed four incomplete sentences, two comma splices, and eight or ten misspellings.

"We can't have this," Dr. Braithwaite said. "Our graduates must *not* write so poorly. It gives my college a bad name, you see."

"I don't recognize the writer's name," I said. "Not one of my students."

"I know that. I'm not saying you are responsible. I'm asking you what we need to do?"

"Well," I said, "we already require a year of composition. After freshman year, though, I doubt whether any teacher marks their grammar or punctuation. Some teachers mark students' spelling errors, maybe."

"What would you do?"

"Do? Me? Well, I suppose I'd give every teacher on campus a copy of the *Harbrace College Handbook*."

I opened my copy of *Harbrace* and showed him the inside cover where the authors had provided a convenient checklist of punctuation and grammar. Here were all the symbols—comma splice, fragment, dangling modifier, YIP (You Illiterate Primate)—and an index showing where to find explanations.

"If every teacher assigned at least one essay during the semester and applied these guidelines from *Harbrace*, students might begin thinking that the college faculty has high standards when it comes to writing. Might make students pay more attention in comp class, too, since more of their grades would depend on it."

"In other words," the director mused, "every teacher on campus becomes an English teacher first."

"Seems reasonable to me," I said. And in the abstract, it did make sense. Then again, I was already an English teacher.

Dr. Braithwaite held general faculty meetings at 7:00 A.M. once or twice a month. A month after our conversation he showed up with a handcart stacked with copies of the *Harbrace College Handbook*. The books were passed out to the faculty while our English department chairman explained them. The director had ordered him to give a short lesson on how to use the correction chart.

"Effective immediately," Dr. Braithwaite announced, "each academic class on campus will require at least one student essay per student. Each will be graded both on content and on mechanics. You will grade grammar and punctuation by the book. Essays will fail if they are flawed. The English faculty will be happy to assist you in learning how to recognize poor grammar and poor spelling, if necessary."

This was followed by a general speech about how all of us had advanced degrees and were professionals in our various disciplines and should expect students aspiring to college degrees to communicate effectively. He might have even used that old gag, "Just think, fore years ago I cudn't even spel enjineer and now I are one!" I noticed that many of our colleagues were glaring at the English chairman. People were mentally sharpening knives and looping hangman's knots. "Must be Rowley's idea" is what they were thinking. The other five members of the English department were trying to remember where they had filed their résumés.

I couldn't blame the science and social science teachers. In many classes in those days grades were simply determined by a set of standard multiple choice exams—most of which could be graded by teaching assistants (or chimpanzees)—which left the professors free to play golf, go fishing, or tinker with their apparatuses in the lab. Looking at student papers was an imposition on their valuable time. One professor had even told me once that he would prefer not to have committee meetings on Wednesday since it could spoil both weekends.

Nothing so endeared me to Dr. Braithwaite as the Slotted Pot Episode. In the spirit of keeping our college a true community of scholars, Director Braithwaite created opportunities for his faculty to mingle and act as a unit. One technique he used was to schedule each department to host an open house that all faculty attended.

During our mandatory tour of the art department we were being led past some shelves on which student ceramics were displayed. I was walking behind Jim Watson of the business department and just ahead of Dr. Braithwaite when we arrived at a slender pot about three feet tall. It had narrow slots running from top to bottom.

"That'll never hold water," Jim remarked. When it came to logic, Watson was a regular Dr. Spock.

"How do you know?" I quipped. "Did you ever *try* it?"

Dr. Braithwaite slapped my shoulder so hard that it nearly sent me to my knees.

"*That's* the kind of thinking I want!" he said.

He made me repeat it for the benefit of the rest of the group. Two weeks afterward when I went to the treasurer's office for my paycheck, I found I had been given a five-dollar raise.

The landscaping of the College of Southern Utah included artificial hills where pine and spruce shaded arrangements of huge boulders. Very, very attractive. But not functional enough for Dr. Braithwaite. Orders were given, and before long three of those conifer groves featured semi-hidden little amphitheaters where a teacher could hold class. My creative writing classes met in these on many a sunny day. A couple of times we even went out there in the snow to sit on the log benches and work on our nature essays.

Another personal mission of the director was to transform his campus into a meeting point between mountains and desert. Behind Cedar City there was a "reef" or cuesta of sandstone of an astonishing red hue, and beyond the red stone cliffs were mountains rising into aspen and conifer forests where clear mountain streams went burbling along over the rocks. Beyond the hills on the other side of town were the upper reaches of the Escalante Desert, punctuated with clusters of bush cedar and piñon trees. Dr. Braithwaite loved to wander these wild places.

One day I went to my classroom to find him and the paint crew foreman waiting for me. Dr. Braithwaite handed me a branch of sagebrush and a Mason jar containing pinkish desert sand. The foreman was holding a large pinecone.

"What do you think of these colors?" he asked.

"Very nice," I replied.

"Your class will meet in the outdoor amphitheater this week," he said.

"Oh."

The students and I returned to the classroom a week later to find that it had been repainted in colors of sage, rich light brown, and pink. As I began to pay more attention I saw that most of the other rooms on campus were also painted some desert or mountain hue. Dr. Braithwaite would hand the paint crew foreman a stone from a riverbed or an aspen leaf and tell him to go paint some classroom or hallway. The effect was to create a campus with a soothing natural feel to it, a place that fit into its geological and botanical surroundings.

Not long after this incident I was watching the nightly television news. A correspondent was showing the results of the latest atomic bomb experiment down at White Sands where the desert sand had been fused into glass. A group of demented scientists were wreaking ecological havoc with a thousand square miles of desert so that a group of equally demented politicians could annihilate one another and leave the planet cloaked in radioactive twilight.

And on our small campus was one man, a man of faith who loved beauty, quietly fulfilling a dream that his college might blend with its environment.

I suppose it was the Gravel Episode that made me realize the full influence Dr. Braithwaite had over his faculty. I think he could get us to do anything.

I had already learned that he once suffered from stress brought on by working himself too hard. He told me about one of several tricks that helped him get over it (besides stealing my desk). He got himself a tall stack of letter trays. Then each morning he made it his routine to sort the previous day's letters, memos, and meeting notices into the trays.

The first half dozen trays were labeled with names—other administrators, secretaries, faculty members. "Dean Schmit can do this" or "Margie can do this" were typical labels. Down the stack a bit further was a tray marked "Any faculty member can do this," while below that one was "This can wait," and at the very bottom was a tray marked "I must absolutely do this myself."

When he began his therapy, the bottom tray was always full. Inside of a year, it was the only tray that was always empty.

Dr. Braithwaite, having finished with his daily duties (if there were any) and having made a phone call or two, would give his secretary some of the remaining memos to distribute. He would then fold the rest into his suit pocket and set off in search of volunteers. I remember one day he stopped me on the sidewalk and reached into his pocket. Handing me a folded letter, he said, "Would you deal with this, please?"

It was a letter from a Salt Lake City newspaper. They were planning an article on budget and faculty positions at CSUtah. Took me three days of research to answer all their questions, but I did it. And Dr. Braithwaite didn't have to.

Another time he handed me a folded memo in which a young teaching assistant was complaining about her treatment in the history department.

"Deal with this, would you, Jim?" Dr. Braithwaite said.

So I went and talked with two or three history faculty, found the young woman and talked with her, and resolved the thing. This, I thought, is how real universities operate, with each person contributing to the good of the whole. (Did I mention that I was *very* young at the time?)

Now to the gravel and the dump truck.

CSUtah had a faculty cabin in the mountains behind Cedar City where various campus groups met for weekend retreats, picnics, and general recreation. The cabin had a small parking lot that was in need of more gravel. Since the cabin was not technically part of the physical campus, the college's physical plant could not work on it. The college could, however, provide the gravel and the weekend loan of a truck.

"See to this, would you?" Dr. Braithwaite said, handing me an intraoffice invoice with which I would procure one large dump truck and two yards of coarse gravel.

"By myself?"

For those of you who don't know, a yard of gravel weighs approximately a ton. A shovelful of gravel weighs between five and eight pounds, so we're talking about maybe three hundred to four hundred shovelfuls to the ton.

"Get Mr. Watson and Mr. McCrimmon to help you. Maybe that tall fellow, Jones."

"Drive a dump truck?" I said.

"Your file shows that you drove a lumber truck and a tour bus, correct?"

As a matter of fact, it was correct. At Estes Park Lumber Company I learned to double-clutch a heavy International with a split rear end. In fact, I could double clutch and split shift at the same time. Later, driving for Panorama Peak Tours, I drove a 6 x 6 Dodge (also with split rear end) as well as a larger dually army truck.

Anyway, Saturday morning arrived.

I went to the motor pool and found the truck, a two-ton Chevy from the 1950s. I struggled with a shift lever that didn't want to move into neutral and a choke control that seemed to lack any actual physical linkage with the engine. Lucky thing I was a Gentile: a good Mormon would probably lack the swear-word vocabulary necessary to operate this piece of machinery.

The engine finally coughed into life after I had pumped the gas pedal sixty-two times while holding back on the choke control with both hands and standing on the starter button. The belch of black soot led the local radio station to report another atomic test blast at White Sands.

I pulled up alongside the gravel pile where my accomplices were waiting with shovels. (In many dictionaries there is a picture of several assistant professors with shovels right next to the word "incongruity.")

Our first idea was to try standing on the gravel pile while we threw shovelfuls of gravel toward the truck. Teachers with long-handle shovels trying to coordinate such a feat was pretty much hopeless. The gravel flew with enthusiasm but without much in the way of accuracy.

"I think that's all she'll hold," Jones remarked, wiping sweat from his brow and wincing as the salty sweat stung his blistered palm.

"Yeah, we pretty much got the cab full," I observed, "not to mention the space between the cab and the truck bed. Now we ought to put some in the back."

Ever the logical one, Watson observed how most of our physical energy was being expended throwing gravel across a distance of more than fifteen feet. For every shovelful we managed to land inside the truck, another one went over it entirely and one clattered against the side. This explained why the truck wasn't yet full even though our backs were sore and our hands were blistered.

Maybe we could move the truck closer to the pile, Watson said.

I had an even better idea. I'd back the truck *into* the pile.

Two of us used most of our remaining strength to lower the tailgate, a plate of solid steel that might have been salvaged from the battleship USS *Utah*, thick enough to turn a ten-inch artillery shell. When we unhooked the latches, it came down with a crash that shoved the truck forward several yards.

I got into the cab and told my Mormon colleagues to cover their ears lest they be corrupteth while I sworeth the engine into running again. As soon as the exhaust cloud cleared enough for me to see the controls, I put the gearbox through a horrid cacophony of grinding noises reminiscent of marbles going around in a food blender.

I pulled forward fifty yards or so. Then I reversed toward the gravel pile at high speed, engine whining, clutch smoking, and dual tires throwing dirt. And I must say that whatever may be their shortcomings in the fine art of swearing, Mormons are remarkably agile.

The trick of crashing the back of the truck into the pile of gravel worked very well, if I do say so myself. We were now able to shovel two tons of rock into the truck in just under three hours, leaving us plenty of time to figure out how we were going to close the tailgate. All four of us couldn't budge it, partly because of its weight and partly because there were stones jammed between the tailgate and truck bed and partly because between us we couldn't have lifted a full can of Coors by then. If there had been a can of Coors in Cedar City.

"Maybe we could use that tractor over there to lift the tailgate," suggested McCrimmon.

"*What* tractor?" I asked.

"That one. Right there." He pointed. "The one with the front end loader on it."

4

Chasing the Word

The sins of the people upon our own heads if we did not teach them the word of God with all diligence.
Jacob 1:19

"So, what do you guys know about the Word of Wisdom?" I asked. "You know, the Mormon bible? The Book of Mormon? The LDS bible?"

It was summer and I was with the U.S. Forest Service again, picking up cigarette butts and pop-tops and cleaning outhouses.

"You mean like in Utah?" Butch said. "Ain't that the scripture that God gave to some guy? I think it's the guy up on the pole there in Salt Lake."

"No, that thing on top of the pillar in Temple Square is a statue of a seagull," I said.

"God gave scripture to a seagull?"

"No, no!" Steve said. "You got it all wrong. There was a Mormon came to the house once and told us all about it."

"Wait a minute. Are you asking us to believe that a Mormon actually came to your house?"

"Yup. Right up to the front door."

"Holy Moses."

"No, Moses is that Hebrew guy with the stone tablets. Didn't you see that movie about the Ten Commandments? This guy up on the pole—"

"I thought it was a seagull."

"You gonna let me finish this story, or am I goin' to show your head how to inspect the vault under this outhouse?"

"Go ahead."

"So this guy they made a statue to, he's an angel, see? He shows up at the farm of this guy, I think his name's Smith or somethin', and he gives him a golden shovel."

"You're thinking of the golden spike," I said.

"You ain't gonna learn nuthin' if you keep interruptin' me. Now, where was I? Oh, yeah. This angel gives Smith a gold shovel and he says, 'Go cultivate your garden.'"

"That was Voltaire. In *Candide*."

"You know what, Work? You are *way* overeducated. So Smith, he goes out in the garden and digs around and comes up with these copper plates with a bunch of writin' on 'em, only nobody can read it. So he writes it all out and that's where the Mormons got their bible. That's what the missionaries told me."

"If nobody could read it, how could he write it?"

"Well, hell, Steve! You could *write out* Chinese without readin' it, couldn't you?"

"I guess."

"I've got a question," I put in. "How is it you can quote Voltaire, sort of?"

"My high school teacher made me memorize it."

During the first year in Cedar City we kept hearing allusions to what seemed to be a set of rules for everyday living. Don't eat meat unless it's dead, don't look a gift house in the foyer, stuff like that. The allusions came from waitresses when we asked for the wine list, from the checkout lady at the grocery where we bought our meat and coffee, and from LDS students who caught a stale whiff of pipe tobacco emanating from my tweed jacket. Neither Sharon nor myself knew what they were talking about, but don't be too hard on us. We were not discriminating against the LDS church when it came to ignorance of their religion. We didn't know much about any religion. I didn't know that Catholics had to sit through sermons—I figured it was Scots Presbyterians who came up with that particular punishment—and I believed that Baptists couldn't be Baptists unless they got undressed in front of everybody and cannonballed into a big tank of water.

You know how your English teacher taught you to figure out the meaning of a word by looking at its context? That's what we did when we heard people say "word of wisdom." We deduced from the context that you should not consume tobacco, caffeine, or alcohol, nor should you cuss, covet, crave, or cosign a loan application. At least that's what Gene Woolf told me one day over coffee. About the loan application, I mean.

I know what you're thinking.

You're thinking, Why didn't you just ask somebody what "Word of Wisdom" meant?

I could have asked pretty near anybody I saw. You see, CSUtah's student body was 90 percent Latter-day Saints. (And of approximately one hundred faculty, only six or seven were not members of the LDS church.) As a bonus, at least half of that 90 percent belonged to an exclusive, indomitable fraternity known as "returned missionaries." Missionaries are usually young people who volunteer to spend two years traveling among the heathen Gentiles where they tell them about Mormonism and support the company that makes bicycle tires. As faculty advisor to the campus newspaper, the *Thunderbird*, I enjoyed a weekly locking of horns with a conservative, militant student editor who was a returned missionary. In his case I assumed the term "returned" meant he had been sent back from some country demanding a replacement.

So why not ask some missionary about the Word? Well . . .

When I went into a local bookstore and asked to buy a copy of a book that could be found free in any hotel room in Utah or obtained simply by standing on any busy intersection in Logan or Provo and whispering, "I need a Book of Mormon," the salesperson looked at me with understandable suspicion. Then the salesperson recognized me from the picture accompanying a newspaper article about new faculty. You'd have thought I'd been smoking in their restroom or something.

It turned into a standoff—this clerk did not want to risk selling me the Holy Tome, and I did not want to look even *more* suspicious by sneaking out of the store. The standoff was interrupted when a smallish and oldish female person came huffing up to the cash register.

"I want a Bible," she demanded.

"This one has been popular," the salesperson said, drawing forth a copy of the recently modernized *Good News for Modern Man.*

"Not that one!" shrieked the crone, slamming the desk with her shillelagh. "I *want* the King James version, just the way Christ wrote it! What's the matter with you people, anyway?"

That was enough for me, and so I left. In those days empty motel rooms were rarely locked, and motel copies of the Book of Mormon have very durable bindings.

I'm a literature person.

I especially love literary archaeology, literary mysteries, and stories behind the writing of books. When I heard that Joseph Smith had seen metal plates inscribed with biblical texts, I became very curious. When I read that other men had witnessed the plates and that the plates had vanished, I was hooked. Had to know more. However, when I asked my colleagues and neighbors for information, it was as if I had asked them about their sex lives.

"Oh, Joseph Smith the prophet? Ah. Well, you need to ask a real scholar about him. Like a bishop maybe."

"You want to know about the Mormon Tabernacle? Well, that's where the choir rehearses. As for the temple, it's sort of like your church, see."

Sort of like *my* church?

You mean that if I were to go inside that soaring cathedral of flying buttresses and gothic arches in stone, that magnificent tribute in marble and granite to the Infinite Power, I would find asphalt tile floors and hard benches illuminated by the dim yellow light coming in through plain glass windows? Like in my church?

Seemed hard to believe.

A literature teacher of my acquaintance couldn't tell me much about the Latter-day Saints, and he and his ancestors "wuz one." The local druggist didn't know "nuthin' special about it." I tried to engage the milkman in a religious conversation, but apparently he was under orders to deliver the milk and keep moving.

So I realized that I would have to turn to the most unlikely source of knowledge imaginable: college students.

I'll tell you something about my own preparation for a religiously centered life, and I know for a fact that it represents the vast majority of my Protestant peers. My early religious training came from memorizing bits of scripture to earn prizes. From there I graduated to watching Mr. Patrickson arrange little cloth cutout dolls on an easel covered with felt. The prize system was a great disappointment, as far as pedagogical method was concerned, and I lost interest in it. My brother memorized a Bible passage and was rewarded with a miniature "hurricane lamp" that consisted of a miniature candle inside a small glass chimney on a little round bit of wood. He could light the candle and walk around with it like a lantern, although we discovered it wasn't much good for reading comics underneath the bedcovers.

My turn came the very next year of Saturday Bible school. I memorized the passage about the Lord being a shepherd and me not wanting for anything, but it wasn't true. I wanted one of those hurricane lamps with the little candle inside. My prize, however, turned out to be a pencil with the Twenty-third Psalm printed on it.

What the heck was *this*?

A lousy pencil? One biblical fact I had picked up from my father, or possibly my grandfather, was that if you disrespect the Bible in any way whatever, whether you put something down on top of it (let's say a bottle of Coke, just as a hypothetical example that might have earned me a fifteen-minute lecture) or tore a page or (gasp!) *wrote* in it, the heavens would open and a really angry angel with a flaming sword would come down to cleaveth and rendeth thee forthwith and horridly.

And so now I owned a pencil upon which was printed the same verse I had already *memorized*, and if I tried to sharpen it so as to actually use it as a pencil, the avenging angel would smiteth the hell out of me the instant the pencil sharpener reached the phrase "The Lord is . . ."

Besides Bible school and Sunday school (where we found out that the Bible was full of fairly undecipherable verses and that David and Joshua and Adam and Peter were all the same little felt doll with different colored turbans) we had Cecil B. DeMille. Thanks to him we filled in our theological knowledge in quick order. Apparently, the Bible, if you could get through the secret codes of thees and thys and theretofores wherewith, was chockablock full of tales of swordplay, grand battles, close encounters with invisible beings, and scantily clad women. The heroes usually didn't wear shirts. They rode around in neat chariots and looked like Victor Mature unless they looked like Charlton Heston. Heston was an Egyptian, apparently, until he turned into a Hebrew. And Victor Mature was either Christian or just looked constipated. We never knew which.

Women in these movies were either swathed to the teeth in long robes, which in the desert climate must have been like walking around wearing a sauna, or else they were wearing filmy little outfits like the girls in the Arabian Nights films. They did a lot of dancing while the men lounged around on huge cushions and drank.

The whole story pretty much boiled down to this: God created two people, both of whom were white and spoke English. He put them in a garden where the most fun they could have was naming things. And let's face it: after you've figured out that an elephant isn't a turtle and a rock isn't a potato, you've got a whole lot of the rest of the day left over.

Our first parents sinned by eating something. Whether apple, apricot, or pomegranate, whatever Adam and Eve ate, they got themselves kicked out of Eden. Supposedly this was a punishment, but my pals and I didn't see it that way. No sooner was the unhappy couple outside the garden than they began begetting. Right off the bat they begat boys who invented weapons (any boy's first delight). Pretty soon there was a whole tribe of the begotten. According to the movies, they all got to eat meat and drink liquor and watch dancing girls who wore nothing but that sheer stuff our mothers used to hang in the windows under the drapes.

Fighting seemed to be OK with God, as long as it was about him. Drinking was obviously OK, or else the angel with the flaming sword would cleaveth and woundeth those bearded guys who lounged around on cushions with pitchers of wine. Buying slaves wasn't much of a sin, especially if you were kind to them and let them build obelisks and rule Egypt and stuff. Taking over territory, that was a good thing. And if you got a chance to watch a female in her bath, by all means have at it. You should try to be a good Samaritan (or was it that you should be good *to* a Samaritan whenever you run across one?), and if you're not catching any fish, throw the net on the other side of the boat.

This last one ran counter to the wishes of the Colorado Fish and Wish Commission. A warden confiscated our net and told us we were limited to one pole with no more than two treble hooks. Good thing we never had to feed fish to the Five Thousand.

The afternoon we learned about Goliath's untimely end we fell over each other in a rush to make slings. And the Bible is right: an average ten-year-old with a sling about, oh, eighteen inches long can hurl a small stone a hundred yards or through the (closed) kitchen window, whichever comes first.

We did think Goliath was pretty dumb because he didn't see the rock coming in time to duck—even my friend Gary had the presence of mind to duck my stone, although my other friend Jimmy Three Eyes didn't—but that's a topic we may get to later in the section concerning Darwin and the Survival of the Fittest. Or Fastest.

Jimmy had a cornet, I had a bugle that some relative had carried up San Juan Hill, and one of the guys, I think it might have been Gary, had a trombone. Early one morning we lined up at McGrouser's old cinder-block house to see if there was anything to this Jericho story. I can report only that Jericho was probably not surrounded by cinder-block walls and that Old Man McGrouser was definitely not a supporter of Bible research. Not like Harriett's mother, who actually suggested that we go read the Old Testament again after we cut Harriett's favorite doll in half. Turned out to be a misreading of scripture, that's all.

I won't say that *all* my adolescent theological training stayed with me, but I think I retained more of it than my students did. After attaining teacherhood I was often reminded of the average college student's biblical ignorance. "What does the Bible say about suicide?" I'd ask. "Huh?" came the reply. "OK, name the Seven Deadly Sins." Most students were up to speed on gluttony and lust but didn't know if avarice and covetousness were the same thing.

"Can anybody name the Seven Cardinal Virtues?"

Well, there's paying your bills on time, yielding to pedestrians in a crosswalk, and wearing clean underwear in case of an accident. Most of my students couldn't even name the Seven Dwarves. Let's see, Grumpy, Donner, Blitzen . . .

It came as no surprise to discover that the average college student in Utah had paid as little attention in church class as those in the world of Gentiles. Either they didn't know the answers to my questions or pretended ignorance so they wouldn't have to answer. One day in literature class, however, I was describing scholars' efforts to establish the original text of *Beowulf* when I realized I had an opportunity staring me in the face. And this time it wasn't Marty Kean in her leotard.

"Without the original Old English or Norse version," I said, "we can't be sure our interpretations are correct. It's like the situation we see in the plates revealed to Joseph Smith. Let's see . . . there were three sets of writings in that case? Who can tell me about Mr. Smith?"

One student began to answer, only to be pummeled by fists from both sides.

"I thought you meant Mr. Smith in the ceramics department," he said as he rubbed his sore shoulder. "Sorry."

So. The conspiracy to keep me ignorant extended into the ranks of freshmen and sophomores. No one would tell me anything, not even my friends of the Coffee Shop Tontine. There was an iron wall of secrecy surrounding the scriptures. Back in Colorado I couldn't sit down to lunch without two Mormon missionaries ringing the doorbell. Here in the heart of LDS territory I was on my own when it came to learning anything about the Book of Mormon.

5

The Big House

Thou shalt not covet thy neighbor's house.
Mosiah 13:24

Remember "synchronicity," one thing leading on to another in meaningful coincidences? Well, here we go again. Things in Cedar City, Utah, were beginning to take on some very suspicious connections.

That first house we rented, which seemed to be the only available one in Cedar City, not only came with gaps in the walls that let sunshine come streaming through and a yard of drifting sand dunes that attracted every cat within six blocks. It also came empty. We would need a houseful of furniture, and we would need it before the motel room bill ran headlong into the house lease.

"How's the house hunting coming along?" Chairman Rowley asked.

"Found one," I said. "But it's unfurnished. I need to get a houseful of furniture if we're going to live there."

Chairman Rowley looked thoughtful and wrote himself a note.

The next day the phone in the motel room rang.

"Mr. Work? This is Harold over at Valley Vista Furniture. Understand you need a houseful of furniture?"

"Yes?"

"What are we talking about here? Kitchen, living room?"

"And bedroom. Three beds, at least. Dressers. Couch. I'd like a desk."

"Come on out. We'll see what we can do."

And thus followed what could be the most bizarre bit of haggling I've ever experienced. Harold turned out to be a mid-thirties guy with good looks, a Clark Gable mustache, a double-breasted suit, and an eye for the ladies. You just know from the way some men see an attractive woman passing by and they walk into the wall that they have an eye for ladies. Less of an eye for obstacles.

He had already worked out a set of furniture for us. There was a couch and easy chair he had been trying hard to get rid of and could mark way down for us. I saw the problem with the set: the nubbly fabric was the color of coffee (or tobacco spit) and so naturally no LDS would want it. There was a mismatched end table—mismatched because it was designed around a fake wagon wheel that no self-respecting furniture maker would ever *try* to match—a low table that he refused to put a term to until I remarked that "back home" in Gentile country we called them "coffee tables" or "cocktail tables"—with matching end table. He had a kitchen set ("very slight damage") and a nice set of bunk beds ("not much call for them") and a double bed.

I immediately began to haggle as my bride looked on.

"How much?" I said.

Sharon beamed proudly at my bargaining expertise. She had that "wanna neck?" look in her large brown eyes.

"How much?" the salesman said. "Well, what kind of monthly payments can you make?"

"Huh? Oh, we figured about forty dollars."

He was going to start at two hundred, I figured. Maybe by beginning with a ridiculous offer he'd take pity on my innocence and come down to $180.

"Forty?" he said.

"OK, OK," I answered. "You drive a hard bargain. Forty-five."

"Forty-five?" He took a piece of folded paper from inside the double breasted suit coat and studied it. "Forty-five," he repeated, mostly to himself.

I was about to say fifty when he beckoned for us to follow him to a corner of the store where a hanging sign announced that DÉCOR was to be found there. He stopped next to a pile of brass rods and Naugahyde.

"Nesting footstools," he explained. "Comes apart, see? Very modern, very modern."

And indeed, the three squares of shiny brass rods and thin Naugahyde pads were intended to be footstools. Each was only four or five inches high, but there were three of them.

"Great for extra seating," he said.

"I don't know," I said. "I'd have to think it over."

"Oh? Well, hey! Look here at these beanbag chairs! For your little girls! They'd love these!"

One of the beanbags was stuffed vinyl. The other looked like it had been made from seat covers stolen out of a '51 Mercury.

"What do you say?" he pleaded. "We'll include both of these beanbags *and* the footstools. How about this nice jewelry chest for the wife?"

"It's just that we have a tight budget . . ."

I was really haggling now.

"OK," he said. "Two throw rugs. I'll add two throw rugs to the deal."

Sharon was admiring a cobalt blue blown glass flower vase.

"Hey!" Harold exclaimed. "I'll throw that in. Yes. Pretty, isn't it? So, two rugs, the vase, footstools, and beanbag chairs. You can't say no that that, can you?"

"For . . . how much?"

"You said forty-five a month. And payments can start in a couple of months, not right away. Or later. Whatta ya say?"

Driving back to the motel, we puzzled over the whole bizarre deal and wondered what it meant. I was of the opinion that when Harold realized he was dealing with a master of the art of haggling he had simply caved in. Sharon, on the other hand, thought that he was a homeless person who had wandered into the furniture store.

The theory we settled on was this: since we were young and obviously desperate for furniture and had two darling little girls, since we were strangers in town and potential recruits for their church, the store owners were doing this just so they could slowly sucker us into liking them.

Some time later I was chatting with Chairman Rowley again.

"Did you get your furniture?" he asked.

"Yes," I said. "But Harold, he's a strange one. He acted like he'd get discommunicated or circumcised or something if the Works didn't walk out of the store with a truckload of furniture. Personally? I think he was short of his sales quota and his boss was leaning on him."

"Could be somebody leaning on him, for sure," Chairman Rowley said. "So, how's the house?"

"Lots of fresh air," I said. "Even with the windows closed. Sharon says that if we can't find a real house to live in pretty soon, we're going back to Colorado. She's tired of having every little breeze blow the tablecloth into the bathroom."

He went back to his office and closed the door. In a minute I saw the red button on the secretary's phone light up and knew he was making a call.

A week went by, possibly more than a week.

Harold from the furniture store called. Could we meet him at his house? He needed to leave town for a couple of years and would sure like to have reliable renters. He gave me the address. It was only a few blocks away from campus.

"Going on a church mission?" I asked.

"Sort of, yeah," he said.

Harold's house turned out to be a two-story, four-square brick house with artificial white pillars in front. I had walked past it many times on my way to school and assumed it was either a fraternity house, the local library, or a mausoleum. Harold and his dog gave us the tour from the four bedrooms upstairs to the music room, library, and living room downstairs and on into the basement with its two bedrooms, recreation room, and laundry.

"Can't take the dog with me," he said. "But I can come back for him in a month or two. Tell you what, I'll make a deal with you. You take care of the dog until I can come get him, and you can keep the washer and dryer there. Yours to keep. Whatta ya say? What kind of rent would you be willing to pay?"

"Forty bucks a month?" I haggled.

Harold went pale. He looked to the dog for support, but the dog wasn't about to help anyone who would leave him with strangers.

"Actually," Harold whined, "I'd have to get about two hundred."

"One fifty," I said. "I was just kidding with the forty."

"One eighty."

"You got a deal."

Since then I have been in some negotiations where I thought I had some leverage, but never have I experienced anything like being a minority Gentile bargaining with a Mormon ladies' man to whom it has been suggested he move to Provo and repent. I was sorely tempted to mention to Chairman Rowley that I could use a new car and a weekend vacation in Las Vegas.

Know what the whole thing felt like? It felt like the way I used to get summer jobs when I was a kid.

I said earlier that I had never filled out a job application and I was telling the truth. I would inform Dad that I wanted a summer job, and after we revived him with smelling salts he'd say something like, "Well, maybe you ought to talk to Ken at the Conoco station. Or maybe Dick at the Piggly Wiggly store." A day or two later I would walk in and get the job. It was always at some business where Dad was a good customer. Dad never suggested that I go to work for him in the plumbing shop that he owned, however.

Having previously confessed to hosting clandestine cocktail parties in the basement of Harold's big brick house, I might as well cleanse my soul by telling the whole rest of the story.

Although the cocktail parties were often nothing more than beer gatherings where some guests brought their own noncaffeinated soda pop, getting the affair organized could have qualified as field experience for undercover agents.

It would usually begin on campus where I knew one or two people who would accept a free drink. When we felt like having a party, I would waylay one of these sinners and whisper, "Sharon and I are thinking of a party at our house."

"Who else have you told?"

"Just you, so far."

"Good. Leave it to me. I'll get Bill. Roy and his wife can come, probably. Lawrence's wife is out of town all next week, so he's a good bet. Laura, I'm not sure. Maybe if someone will give her a ride. A Mormon bishop lives in your neighborhood, and if he sees her car outside your house . . . well, you know."

"I do?" I whispered. "He'd think she was having an affair with me?"

"Worse. He'd think she was proselytizing you."

"My God."

"Yes, he does come into it. You do know what proselytizing means, don't you?"

"I'm not real clear on it, no. But if Laura does it . . ."

"Let's get back to your guest list," he said. "Peter and Anne can walk over."

"It's a long walk," I said.

"They wouldn't want their car to be seen in front of your house either."

"They could ride their bikes," I suggested helpfully.

"God, no! That would look like you had missionaries."

"Oh."

"Now, we can't be seen carrying any beer or wine, so here's twenty bucks. You'll have to buy it for us. If it costs more, we'll pass a hat at the party. We'll bring everything else."

"What do you people bring to parties?" I asked. "Chips, pretzels, bean dip?"

"No," he confided, looking over his shoulder to make sure no one was listening. "Casseroles."

I will further confess that the Works' secret mission to convert the entire LDS population to the Gospel of Jim Beam went much further than allowing a bunch of sneaks to gather in our basement in order to get soggy on 3.2 beer. Much further, indeed. Remember how I said I had to go to the comptroller's office every two weeks for my paycheck? Keep that thought a minute while I give you a little background.

Things have changed now, but in those days all liquor in Utah was sold through a liquor store owned by the state. There was no sign on the building, no windows with advertising, just a modest doorway in a plain wall with the legend "Utah Liquor Authority" over the door. It was like going in to get license plates for your car, only less exciting.

Once inside, you would look in vain for bottles of booze because they were all stored in the back room. Like the vehicle registration office, the alcohol outlet had one end of the room blocked by a long counter separated with windows like those of bank tellers. Countertops covered with glass stood against the walls; under the glass were typed lists of all the liquor and the prices. A clerk would hand you a clipboard with an official-looking order form listing the inventory and you would check off what you wanted and how much of it. Beer, six-pack, two, Schlitz. Scotch, quart, one, McCallum.

Thrilling as it sounds so far, the fun was just beginning. Now you went to back to a clerk of your own choosing, depending on whether you wanted the grim-faced one or the one with the disapproving frown. To this person you handed your list. And your permit.

Permit?

Oh, yes. Remember, to purchase liquor you needed that state-issued ID card, which meant that the State of Utah not only controlled who bought alcohol, but kept a record of how much you bought and what kind it was. So, you handed the clerk your card. He or she would scrutinize your face, copy the transaction into a ledger, and vanish into the back room to get your drugs—I mean, your alcohol.

Now that you have the picture let's get back to the comptroller's office where I have just signed for my paycheck, perhaps picked up a few dollars in cash for the weekend, and I'm walking down the dimly lit hallway.

A shadowy figure steps out of a dark alcove.

"Work?" the voice whispers.

"Hi, Lawrence!"

"Shut up. Listen, are you going to the liquor store after work today?"

"Thought I might. I want to see if they have any good claret for less than three bucks."

"Listen. Margaret has some relatives coming to visit, see? And they drink. Pick me up a bottle of bourbon and some beer. Better get me about four bottles of wine."

"Sure. Got the money?"

"Can't give it to you here, you dummy! What if somebody saw me giving money to a Gentile? We'll use the usual arrangement."

The Usual Arrangement.

Every month or so it happened that Friday afternoon would find me at the liquor store loading our Ambassador with so many cases of hooch that the back bumper dragged. I had to do it in daylight, too, since the store closed at six o'clock.

With my heavy freight of bottles and cans I'd drive slowly so as not to bottom out in the street crossings. Back home at the brick mausoleum, I'd back into the driveway and unload my cargo into the garage. Except for some free firewood, my bicycle, and Harold's lawnmower, the two-car garage was empty because we didn't own anything. But despite the empty garage, the Ambassador would still sit out in the driveway all night.

That was the signal. Part of the Usual Arrangement.

Remember dorm rooms, where a necktie or coat hanger on the doorknob meant that your roommate was doing some transcendental meditation and you weren't to disturb him until she went home? In Cedar City our green station wagon parked in the driveway after dark meant that I had brought home the booze and it was ready to be picked up. I stacked the stuff just inside the door, usually taking care to sort it according to customer. Then Sharon and I would stay in the house with the TV volume turned way up. Sometimes if we went to bed early we might hear a little creaking sound like somebody opening the side door to the garage. But we never went out to investigate. After all, it could be the police, the phantom missionaries, anybody.

Saturday morning I'd get up, eat my breakfast while my two little girls threw their cereal at me, then get dressed and go outside. If it was summer, I'd haul out Harold's lawnmower to see if I could destroy a few more of his underground sprinkler heads. If it was winter, I'd get his snow shovel and clear the walks. In between seasons there was always drifting sand to be scooped off the driveway. Any of these recreations meant going into the garage. And it would be miraculously devoid of booze. Sometimes there would be a discarded box left behind, probably because the person had carried his liquor away under his coat or in a backpack. And money would be thumbtacked to the wall studs. More money than I had spent. Tens and twenties, usually.

The local banker once remarked to me that most of his bank patrons came in once or twice a month to withdraw cash—"You know, for those little necessities." But he had never seen me take out any cash. This was, of course, long before the ATM. To get your money you either had to go into a bank and by God ask for it or else find a merchant willing to take your check.

"You don't seem to write many checks," he added. "I hope you're not using one of those newfangled credit cards. Very bad habit to get into."

"No," I said. "Wouldn't do that. It's just that I don't ever seem to need much cash. Presbyterians are frugal, you know. Scots Presbyterians."

I wasn't exactly lying. Being a Presbyterian *did* lead people to hand me cash, as long as the state liquor outlet would accept my checks, and Scotch played a role in it.

Did I ever feel bad about helping these good folk acquire mind-altering fluids? Not really. Back in those days, you see, we were aware of only two categories of drinkers. There were what we called "social drinkers" and that included us, people who could go for a month or more without thinking about alcoholic drinks, and "drunks." Drunks were drunk all of the time. Every town had at least one drunk who was an object of pity and also a visual aid for parents lecturing their children on the evils of demon rum.

"Look at him!" they would say whenever they spotted him lurching down the street or sprawled out under a newspaper on the lawn. "That's where liquor leads. Poor soul."

As far as I could tell, the Cedar City fathers never did try to cure their town drunk, probably because he was needed for these object lessons. It was a sad day when he hitched a ride to California with a long-distance Kenworth hauler. They had to borrow St. George's town drunk until they could find a replacement.

"Social drinkers" drink so they will fit into a group. I began drinking 3.2 beer in college because it was what college boys did and I was a college boy. If you chipped in to help buy a pitcher of beer at Sam's Old Town Barroom, you were one of the guys. I didn't particularly like beer, but I liked being in the middle of intellectual conversations. The drinking of Scotch whisky came about because my professor hero, Dr. Zoellner, drank Scotch. I used to let him use my tiny apartment on weekends or whenever I was away on break, and he would show gratitude by leaving a bottle of Scotch on the kitchen counter. I thought it tasted awful. I even put it in coffee, which not only made the Scotch taste even more horrible but ruined the flavor of the coffee as well. Later on I discovered that if I could develop a taste for single malt Scotch I'd be allowed to join a really exclusive group of men (and some women) who'll spend up to a hundred bucks for a quart of liquid that tastes like iodine filtered through a dirty sporran, damages your sinuses and your larynx going down, triggers instant heartburn as it tries to come back up, and leaves you in the morning with the feeling that someone has screwed a #18 C-clamp over your head and the St. Bernard slept with his tail in your mouth.

And then there is wine. The first time it seriously hurt me was when I helped Sharon's Bohemian grandmother polish off a bottle of Mogen David, just so's I'd fit into the family. I can't look at a Mogen David bottle to this very day without feeling my gorge rising. I have a hard time even looking at grapes.

But know your wines and you'll fit in with our gourmet dining club. Drink champagne with us to celebrate graduations, birthdays, Robert Burns's birthday, Cinco de Mayo, and National Grammarians Day. Make your own wine! Build a special room to hold your wine and we'll come to your house to admire it and sample your expensive chardonnays and merlots. And we'll admire you, too, if you happen to be home at the time.

So here in Cedar City I was supplying alcohol-based ammunition to a smallish clique who just wanted to be social with a slightly different group. Oddly, whenever we were invited to an evening gathering where nothing was served that was stronger than Ye Olde Orange Blende, we had just as much fun. And without the throwing up afterward, which was a bonus.

The only time I had second thoughts about being the local bootlegger, the only time I thought that I was perhaps contributing to the delinquency of a Saint, was one Halloween evening when I answered the doorbell to discover one of my friends standing there in a tuxedo and holding a highball glass in his hand.

"Trick or treat!" he said, giggling.

"Honey," I said to Sharon as I closed the door, "you've gotta stop leaving the car in the driveway."

Speaking of cars . . .

I'm sure it will be impossible for my grandkids to read this and believe what a primitive era I lived in. As a graduate student I had never operated any kind of computer. I typed my master's thesis on a rented electric typewriter; the woman whom I paid to type my doctoral dissertation used a rented IBM Selectric. In both cases we had to type an original and four carbon copies (yes, using carbon paper) because Xerox machines did not exist. In my office at CSUtah there was a thing called a ThermoFax that used heat and chemicals to duplicate documents. It took nearly five minutes per page to make a copy, which came out light brown on thin yellowish paper.

No computers, no wireless phones, no cable television, no photocopy machines. No small foreign cars, unless you knew someone who had a fancy MG or a Porsche Speedster. No small cars, period. No, I take it back: there were small cars. Sharon always wanted a little Nash Metropolitan. A Metro would have been just barely big enough to accommodate herself and her goofy male Irish Setter, Shamrock. In Estes Park our music teacher owned a Crosley; it was so small that it only took six football players to pick it up and wedge it sideways into the narrow sidewalk between the variety store and the Dairy Queen. Or five football players and me.

But for the most part, cars were big and heavy. They often had AM radios, but no kind of tape deck, CD player, or FM. Those were unheard of.

Cars were durable, too, as proven by the experience of one of our Cedar City friends. He was on some sort of administrative board, requiring him to make the long drive north once or twice a month. After a few dozen trips up and down the main highway to Logan he decided that it would be quicker to use a gravel country road where state troopers were seldom seen. Using that road he could drive to Logan at a steady 80 mph. Sometimes more. He was doing about ninety, according to his own account, when he noticed that a road grader had been working on the road. The grader had created a mound of dirt and gravel along one edge of the roadway. But the mound kept coming nearer and nearer the edge until it became clear that he would have to cross it if he didn't want to run off the side of the road altogether.

No problem. Well, one problem. There had been a snow, then a thaw, then a freeze. The long mound of graded dirt was frozen.

Not knowing this, he casually steered his Buick into the gravel pile. He was airborne for less than a second and came down still going more than 80 mph with a clear road ahead. Ha! He smiled. More of a bump than he had expected, but he was OK.

Did I mention that it was late at night and that this road runs through a place listed on most maps as the Middle of Nowhere?

The Buick flew on up the road a few hundred yards, stuttered, coughed, and died. It would not restart. He got out with a flashlight and looked in the engine compartment. Nothing amiss. He knelt and shone the light on the muffler. Nothing amiss there either. Maybe something had fallen off when he crossed the gravel pile? Walking back along his tire tracks, his flashlight the only gleam of light for fifty miles in any direction, he came to the source of the problem. The source of the fuel, to be more specific. The Buick had made it over the gravel pile, but the gas tank had not come along for the ride.

I learned a lesson from that story: slow down before you leap. Either that or keep going in spite of everything.

As you know, Utah was originally called the state of Deseret. According to Ernest Taves in *This Is the Place*, "Deseret is a Book of Mormon word signifying honeybee—symbol of industry and frugality." A few years before Sharon and I arrived in Cedar City, Utah's officials went back to that idea and officially adopted "The Beehive State" as an official nickname. We saw pictures of beehives everywhere we went, even on the seal of the State of Utah. It was meant to remind people to keep going, keep working, and keep storing up honey.

Coming from a Scots-Irish farming background, I found the beehive mentality very familiar. Scrape, save, work. Work, scrape, save. Most of all, work. Not long after helping to fill the dump truck with gravel, I learned that there was an excelsior plant just outside town where one could scavenge free aspen wood. The plant cut aspen trees into chunks and shredded the chunks to make packing material. But they couldn't use the butts of the logs, so they gave them away. With only our Nash station wagon and our own energy we stockpiled half a garage full of free firewood.

It provided me with lots of exercise. After loading it and hauling it and unloading it I had to split it with a dull axe that had come to Utah on the Sears and Roebuck handcart. Then I had to stack it in the garage, from whence I would carry it into the house by the armload. I soon learned that aspen burns faster than other wood. In fact, dry aspen burns faster than some types of kerosene. I got so that I could make the 50-yard dash from fireplace to garage in less than thirty seconds so the fire wouldn't burn out while I was bringing more fuel. How we loved those cool evenings, Sharon and our little girls sitting by the fire reading about the Cat in the Hat while Daddy ran back and forth to the garage.

Over time I picked up some humorous anecdotes about the Mormon zest for backbreaking labor and perseverance. One story concerns the time Brigham Young, president of the Latter-day Saints, decided to send men to build a telegraph line westward so Deseret/Utah could communicate with serfs and drones in other kingdoms. The crew foreman sent a wire to Brigham Young:

"Have reached Pacific Ocean. Send instructions."

And Brigham replied, "Bridge it and keep going!"

And the railroad stories. Once again, Brigham Young had sent men into the desert on a mission to link Salt Lake City with the rest of the United States that was cut off from Mormon civilization. Once again the foreman wired the capital:

"Further progress at this time impossible. Temperature 110 in the shade."

Brigham Young's reply: "What are you doing in the shade?"

Or the story of the railroad ties:

"Running out of r.r. ties," the foreman telegraphed. "Move heaven and earth if you have to, but get more ties to us within the month."

"Raised hell," Brigham shot back. "Ties will arrive next week."

Being young and energetic, we seldom spent time sitting in our big house doing nothing. On weekends we would drive out to look at deserts, or up into the mountains, or down to St. George to swim in the hot springs. I also burned off energy by walking to campus whenever my antique English three-speed bike wasn't in working condition.

One evening all of this energy meant that I became the central character in a Cedar City anecdote.

It was the night our station wagon was stolen.

It was a Friday evening and we were thinking of going to Dairy Queen for a chocolate-dipped double swirl or a strawberry sundae. However, when I opened the garage door, all I saw was a stack of aspen butts and a few hundred empty liquor cartons. The Nash had vanished. And we couldn't remember when we had last seen it. Thursday night? I thought I had washed it Thursday night and left it on the driveway to dry.

I phoned the local police and soon both of Cedar City's patrol cars were on the lookout for our green station wagon. Our insurance agent, naturally, was back in Colorado. Fat lot of good he could do us. One of our neighbors offered to loan us his second car until ours was recovered. My student newspaper editor heard of our plight and went prowling the town on his motorcycle hoping to find our Nash and beat hell out of whoever had taken it.

About ten o'clock on Saturday morning we had a phone call from campus security.

"Found your car," the officer said. "And it seems to be OK."

"Great!" I said. "Where did you find it?"

"On campus. The car thief—or thieves—evidently parked it in the faculty parking lot behind Old Main. Right under your office window, in fact."

Brazen outlaws! And then slowly, slowly it dawned on me what had happened. On Friday morning I drove to campus, something I rarely did, and then—as I usually did—I walked home. Having taught for less than two years, I was already on my way to becoming an absentminded professor.

It made a funny story for everyone concerned, of course. The student editor even wrote the story in excruciating detail and published it in the student newspaper. "Absentminded Prof Steals Own Car." But I forgave him. In fact, I even invited him for a drive out into the Escalante Desert the following weekend, just the two of us.

The Nash Ambassador took revenge on me for thoughtlessly abandoning it. Sharon's sister, Susi, had come to stay with us awhile, since the house we had dubbed The Mausoleum had extra bedrooms. Susi brought her baby son with her, a chubby miniature Buddha named Mikey (instantly adopted by our girls as their own personal baby doll). One day Susi and Sharon took the three children to the local drive-in for ice cream, and as Sharon put the Nash's helm hard over to back out of the drive-in, she failed to notice the steel pipe that held the loudspeaker.

Bong. Or rather, boink. Now our lovely, nearly new Ambassador had an unsightly crease in the front fender.

When I saw the damage, I launched myself into a Full-Bore Lateral Monologue on the subject of irresponsibility, looking where you're going, taking care of property, being aware and not chatting with the sister whilst reversing out of parking places. I'm not sure, but I think I also threw in a few references to driving lessons and the need thereof.

Having duly delivered my manly lecture concerning car care and expert driving, I dismissed the ladies with a suggestion that they might retreat to the kitchen where they would do less damage.

Sharon had parked the Ambassador with its rear end facing the garage door so the fender damage would be hidden from the house until she could break the news to me. Not wanting anyone to happen by and see the shameful, careless crease, I thought I would back the car into the garage.

And yes, I remembered to open the garage door. No, I did not accelerate too fast, nor did I forget to release the parking brake. Not trusting the mirror, I opened the driver's side door and looked back, right hand nonchalantly resting on the top of the steering wheel as I skillfully reversed the Ambassador through the doorway.

Almost. What I actually did, while my darling bride and her bemused sister watched from the kitchen window, was to catch the open station wagon door on the doorframe of the garage and bend the aforementioned car door back along the left (and up until now undamaged) front fender.

"Aha!" intoned the Love of My Life, "so pride doth goeth before a fall!"

But aha herself! What Proverbs 16:18 *really* says is, "Pride goeth before destruction, and a haughty spirit before a fall." So there.

Machines and manly pride, now that I think about it, seem to go hand in hand. And transcend any other differences that might exist between Gentile and Mormon. I'm thinking specifically of a certain power saw.

I could be misremembering, but it seems to me it was Jim Watson, the Einstein of the gravel pile, who had purchased this particular piece of infuriating technology. He invited me one weekend to go with him into the cedar breaks outside of town to cut some piñon and cedar firewood.

"Aspen is all right but burns so darn fast," he explained.

"Really?"

"But out on the BLM land we can cut as much dead piñon and cedar as we want."

"All I've got is Harold's antique axe and a bow saw," I whined.

"Not to worry. I've got a reciprocal chainsaw. We'll have a full load of firewood before noon."

That evening I puzzled over what a "reciprocal" chainsaw might look like. Did it have a chain studded with sharp teeth, like a regular chainsaw, except the chain somehow lashed out and drew back? Maybe it was an ordinary chainsaw except that when it worked it expected you to give something back to it. Ah, I had it! He had given one of his friends some tool or other, like a welder or a compressor, and the friend had reciprocated by giving him a chainsaw.

That explains it, I thought as I drifted off to sleep. I just hope to heck it's a decent one, like a Stihl or Husquavarna. I hate borrowing somebody's Homelite.

If this motorized digit remover had been given to Watson in reciprocation, whatever he had given to get it must have been either stolen, radioactive, or on OSHA's top-ten list. When we got to the breaks prepared to do some serious logging, he hauled it out and showed it to me.

Believe it or not, it was actually reciprocal. Whereas normal chainsaws have a toothed flywheel on the side of the engine, this one had an eccentric crank. The pin sticking out of the crank engaged a hole in the back end of a two-foot-long crosscut blade. This crosscut blade slid in and out along a steel backbone. In other words, the saw blade reciprocated.

"Give 'er a try," Watson said, handing me the thing.

The weight was surprising. Imagine holding a bowling ball with a skinny saw blade sticking out of it. That's it. No weight to the blade at all.

"Nice," I said, feeling my right rotator cuff starting to disengage. I pushed the switch to "on" and yanked the starter cord.

Unfortunately, it started. And started moving. Even before I touched the throttle trigger I could see the cutting teeth and rakers of the blade moving back and forth with sinister intent, reaching out for a mouthful of my pants leg.

Holding it straight out in front of me, I waddled toward a fallen piñon. Watson's mouth was moving, but I couldn't hear him. Either his saw was a trifle noisier than most I have used, or a flight of B-52 bombers was passing over on its way to bomb the lizards at White Sands. His mouth puckered, then grimaced. Pucker, grimace. "Wha? Eee? Watts eek?"

He was pointing. At the blade, which at the touch of the throttle had become a blur. The vibration was shaking my fillings loose and blurred my eyesight, but I would have sworn he was pointing at the blade.

"Vas ist? Wash ice? Oh! Watch it! Yeah!" I smiled and nodded. "Sure does go, don't it!"

The vibration had numbed my right hand, and the numbness was climbing up my forearm and heading for my bicep. At least it would soon kill the pain in my rotator cuff.

Problem one: Balance.

With all of its weight in the engine, and the handle strategically placed in order to put all of that weight behind the operator's fist, there was nothing to hold the blade down in case one should hit, for instance, a knot. Of which there are plenty in both piñon and cedar. Or hit the wood grain at the wrong angle. Or touch the tip of the blade to the wood before touching the back of the blade, back near the bucking hooks.

Gingerly I stretched my arms out to put the whizzing reciprocal blade against the log. Alarmingly I felt the blade rise into the air not unlike a French guillotine welcoming its next guest, and cowardly I let go of the handles and executed a *pirouette de petite pas* into a nearby specimen of Spanish bayonet.

"Great saw, huh!" Watson exclaimed. "Lotta power in that engine!"

I asked where it was manufactured, not because I wanted one but because I thought I might do a service to mankind by leveling the factory.

Problem two: Sharpness.

Any manly man will tell you that a chainsaw with as few as one dull tooth can make sawing much less pleasurable than it otherwise is. Dull a tooth or nick a tooth while cutting a hard knot, or a bit of gravel embedded in the log, or, more likely in my case, the metal tailgate of your pickup, and you spend the rest of the day trying to keep the saw from cutting in a curve. Nick enough teeth and your chainsaw will actually go down into the log, curve, and come back up to leave a notch.

But at least the chain keeps going 'round and 'round, spreading any normal dulling out along all the teeth. In the case of Watson's saw, all the cutting took place on the ten or twelve teeth nearest the engine. Back and forth, back and forth. And then it was dull. So you start cutting with the tip, which once again leads you into the pirouette de petit pas mentioned earlier (which translates as "this sucker is about to spin around and leave your paws smaller than they were when you picked it up").

One piece of log cut to length, we then started another one, handing the saw back and forth like a well-rehearsed team.

"You take it."

"My arm's numb. You take it."

"Bullmuffins. *Both* my arms are dead. You take it."

"How long will it take to fill the truck?"

"At this rate? A month, maybe more."

"I don't suppose you've got any beer in the truck?"

"Mormons don't drink beer."

"No, Mormons don't buy beer. There's a difference."

And so on we worked and on we joked into the evening, the saw roaring and the blade sliding back and forth across the piñon as we gradually burned our way through a few more logs. Sure, I kidded him about his tool. He kidded me about not knowing how to operate a genuine reciprocal chainsaw. I kidded him about being a Mormon who liked to drink other people's beer. He kidded me about being an alcoholic, nicotine-addicted, caffeine-swilling nonbeliever condemned to everlasting purgatory. I laughed and said that the well-known generosity of Mormons and my special standing as a community Gentile would lead him to give me more than my share of the firewood, and he laughed right back and said that his Mormon sense of generosity was the only thing keeping him from leaving me afoot in the cedar breaks with the imprint of his boot on my butt.

He offered to sell me his saw, and I suggested he put it where it would require surgical removal, and so we laughed and joshed our way back into town, proud of our masculine instinct for mechanics and glad that unloading the firewood wasn't going to take very long.

6

Shine and a Haircut, Two Bits

(See Judges 16:17–22; John 13:1–20)

Throughout my senior year of college and for the two years of graduate school afterward we never seemed to lack for people with whom to socialize. For one thing, we were all pretty much broke and needed other couples who thought a fine evening's entertainment consisted of listening to LP records on somebody's stereo turntable and sharing beer and potato chips. If one couple could afford a package of franks and the other couple had some buns, it was time for a picnic in the park. If somebody had to move furniture and appliances from one apartment to another, they could count on a dozen rowdy "helpers" to show up. And any kind of academic success such as getting a B+ on a paper in Dr. Zoellner's class or being awarded a $50 scholarship called for our social circle to go all out: Fritos, bean dip, and screw-top bottles of Ripple wine for everybody.

Cedar City social life couldn't hope to match the excitement of crashing in beanbag chairs to hear the latest New Christy Minstrels LP album while the host projected 35 mm slides on a bed sheet, but we certainly didn't feel excluded. Sure, the

Mormons did gather for LDS Family Nights and to play basketball without us, but we were invited to our share of noncocktail parties, non-Coors picnics, and faculty/student mixers that were just non, period.

I've never enjoyed playing contact sports. In fact, as soon as a bunch of guys who had chosen me to be on their football team found out that I would consistently hand the ball to any opponent who even looked as if he might hit me, I was usually relegated to fetching refreshments. I also remember the time back in college when my friends decided not to let me keep on being referee.

"Hey, Ref! Foul!"

"What?"

"Bart clipped me from behind, then Bubba held my head, and Stan kicked it so I'd let go of the ball."

"Sorry. I didn't see it. What's the penalty?"

"How about jail time? Fifteen yards, you idiot."

"Let's see . . . toward their goal or yours?"

"Go find us some Cokes, Work."

In Cedar City I was invited to play in the faculty flag football tournament and found out that I actually enjoyed chasing after other grown men while trying to rip ribbons from their butts. Being uncertain of the ramifications of the game, however, whenever a man headed for me with a gleam in his eye, I just pulled off my own ribbon flags and handed them to him.

A student group had recently discovered a grand old European style of carnage known as "rugby" and three of my students—to whom I had given Ds on a recent test—invited me to be the only faculty member on their team. But I demurred. For one thing, rugby players take pride in telling you that they eat their dead.

For another thing, I don't even give blood at the Red Cross. I had nearly flunked these three clowns and I knew revenge when I saw it coming at me wearing spiked shoes.

Sharon found her own fun with blood. We were at a noncocktail LDS party swilling Orange Crush punch and getting giddy on 7Up floats when Professor Wes Larsen and Sharon struck up a conversation about biology. He was probably arousing her female urges with descriptions of his research, which seemed to involve dosing huge Japanese beetles with radiation to discover how many irradiated bugs it took to equal a 60-watt light bulb. Luring her with graphic romantic terms such as "microscope," "autoclave," "microtome," and "hanging drop slides," he got her to agree to become his laboratory teaching assistant.

And that's where blood and football come in again. Whether it was Dr. Larsenstein or his lovely assistant who came up with the concept I do not know, but the idea was to prick each student's finger and smear a drop of blood on a microscope slide so they could marvel at all the wigglies and squigglies living within their veins and arteries. This innocent exercise was to involve several members of the football team who had to take Biology 101 in order to stay eligible, thus making them captive victims of my wife's instincts for torture and pain.

"Mr. Work!" cried Bubba one day, coming into my class holding forth his wounded digit for me to see. There was indeed a wound on it. Or maybe it was one of those tiny red spider mites. Hard to tell. It seemed miniscule in proportion to Bubba, who was large enough to lean against both sides of a doorframe simultaneously.

"Who hurt you, Bubba?" I asked sympathetically.

"Your wife, Mr. Work! She scares me! She came at me with that needle!"

Sharon later confirmed his story. Bubba and several other of the Mighty Thunderbird linebackers, hulks who would charge into a living wall of two-hundred-pound barbarians in order to protect a lopsided pigskin sphere, found themselves backed into a wall, their eyes wide with fright, defending themselves with lab stools and Bunsen burners. They were terrified by a petite, pretty brunette who stood all of five foot two in her penny loafers and weighed 110 soaking wet and carrying the dog.

"Needles scare you that much?" I asked.

"It's her! She smiles at me!"

"The fiend!" I said. "Next time try shutting your eyes. And don't cry."

"OK, Mr. Work. If you say so. But she made Harry pass out."

Sharon confirmed this. Harry was one of the students whose finger she pricked in the lab. He had gone all rubbery and woozy and had to sit down. Then again, Harry was only an all-state quarterback and not as tough as the other guys.

If you're getting the idea that we felt as though we were part of the community, you're right. Our friends back in the outside world would fear for us if they knew we were sharing Orange Crush and canned-tuna casseroles with these shadowy saints who plotted dark things in secret meetings, who wore ritualistic costumes—or at least perforated undershirts—and who lay awake nights in fear of avenging angels coming to burn them at the stake for drinking caffeine or (gasp!) alcohol. Our friends back home were wrong. Almost as if Cedar City were part of a normal world of friendly interaction, I was allowed to help pour concrete sidewalks on more than one occasion. They welcomed me onto the Arts and Humanities bowling team (mostly due to my incredible high handicap and my ability to terrorize the other team by sending my ball careening down their alley instead of ours). We went wood cutting together. One weekend I was part of a platoon of experts who volunteered to sit on a neighbor's lawn and drink his 7Up while watching him attempt to install piston rings in his '41 Pontiac.

All good camaraderie, which I enjoyed. When it came to the shoeshine episode, however, I was left a trifle nonplussed.

If I could recall the name of the dean of students, I would probably use it and damn the consequences. So I'll call him Dean because he was one, and like James Dean and Dean Stockton, this guy was handsome enough to be in movies. I remember standing around with Sharon, Dean, and his wife at an outdoor student function one day and every time an attractive co-ed happened by, she would flash him a big smile.

"Doesn't that bother you?" I asked his spouse. "I know Sharon gets miffed whenever a lovely co-ed smiles and says hello to me on the street."

"When did that ever happen?" Sharon asked.

Dean's wife laughed it off.

"I knew he was good looking when I married him," she said. "And after all, one shouldn't marry a soldier if one doesn't like parades."

Sometime in the first few months of my time at CSUtah I was more or less at loose ends and found myself walking the halls looking for somebody to talk to. As it happened, Dean's door was open and he was alone, so I invited myself in for a chat. You never knew—someday I might find an office where there was a contraband coffee maker hidden in the closet.

Dean had the bottom drawer of his desk open and his foot on it. He was polishing his shoes.

"That's what I need," I said lightly.

For the children in my readership I should explain that this was a time when male students wore slacks and sport shirts, female students wore skirts, and faculty were expected to wear coats and ties. Except for the ladies, whose garb I intend to describe elsewhere. With coat, tie, and slacks, it was only natural to wear either brown or black leather shoes. No one wore flip-flops, sneakers, shorts, cutoffs, tank tops, or blue jeans to class, and that included the students.

So, I was in Dean's office wearing my brown dress shoes that matched my brown dress slacks and my brown jacket and brown tie. But dress shoes worn as everyday footwear tend to become scuffed, scratched, dusty, and dull. One knew the trick, of course, of wiping each shoe alternately on the back of one's trouser leg, which sort of restored the luster of the shoe but left an odd dirt pattern just behind one's knee. A better trick was Dean's idea of keeping a small shoeshine kit in the bottom desk drawer.

"Pull up a chair," Dean said, smiling. "Stick your foot up here."

"Huh?"

"Put your foot up here. So, how do like our campus so far? Classes going well?"

"Huh?"

Dean pulled a chair over to the desk, pushed me into it, and grabbed my left leg to rest my foot on his drawer. He went to work with a dubbing brush and polishing cloth, all the while making chatty conversation as if he were not a good-looking young guy rubbing his hands all over my foot. With the office door open.

"Listen, thanks and all that," I stammered. "But I do need to get going."

"Nah," he said. "You don't have class until two this afternoon. Tell you what, I'll get these shoes shined and we'll go get lunch together, how's that sound?"

Weird, I thought. I've known men who wouldn't tell another man his fly is open because, well, you know, it's close to Down There. A woman might pick a microscopic bit of lint from a man's lapel, but another man wouldn't reach out to flick a deceased rodent off of another male's tuxedo. When your average American male physically interacts with another male, it's usually during a conflict involving inflated pigskin.

Someone did wander into Dean's office while he was fondling my shoes, though I don't remember who it was. He or she seemed to see it as normal, though. Dean of students, handsome enough to have a right to be arrogant, shining my shoes because he had a shoeshine kit in his desk and my shoes needed a little polish. After leaving CSUtah I spent many hours in the company of associate deans, associate vice presidents, and associate vice associates, and yet I never met one who would shine my shoes. If I had ever suggested it, I would have ended up on the Endangered Assistant Professor list.

The haircut was another example of the same sort of thing. The Mormon people were supposed to be the cliquish closed society and we were supposed to be outsiders, both of us supposed to be suspicious of the other, or the other way around.

Some friends named Tony and Linda came to the house one night. We made pizza from one of those kits you could buy at the grocery store. Cheap wine was involved too. As the evening wore on and the kids were put to bed, we adults were gathered in the kitchen just chatting away about not much in particular. I think Tony was saying something about a suspected coven of polygamists living in Colorado City in a place called the Arizona Strip. Linda, a beautician, was entertaining us with anecdotes from her beauty parlor.

Linda and Tony and Sharon and I were sitting on stools at our breakfast counter. Linda had been looking at my haircut. I had had that particular haircut for approximately the last twenty-three years, or ever since I was old enough to sit on the board laid across the armrests of the barber's chair. Jack Clark, our Estes Park barber, told my dad that I had a "really serious cowlick problem back here" and that he'd fix it by "styling" my hair with a part on the right. No extra charge. I never did care for the mental image associated with the term "cowlick."

Because of this cowlick, imaginary or not, I subsequently showed up at some barber shop every two or three weeks and gave the same instructions. "Clippers all the way around, trim the sideburns, and part it on the right." No barber back then ever shampooed your hair (assuming you washed it before coming to his shop), and when he was finished shortening your hair "all the way around," or as my mother liked to phrase it, "lowering your ears," he would rub in a generous helping of hair oil. You had your choice of rose oil, which had the consistency of Italian dressing and smelled like your grandmother's clothes hamper, or Wildroot, which was thick enough to pack wheel bearings with, smelled like vanilla extract gone bad, and left a stain on the wallpaper behind the couch. Some of those Wildroot stains went deep enough to be seen on the aluminum siding outside.

"I don't like your hair parted that way," Linda suddenly said.

"Oh?" I suddenly replied. "So whatta you gonna do about it?"

Did I mention that wine might have been involved?

"I've got some clippers and a comb in the car. Let me fix it for you."

"Why not?"

Now, any alert reader who has ever had their hair "done" will instantly come up with at least two dozen answers to the question "why not?" but none of them occurred to me at the time. So I soon found myself wrapped in an old bed sheet and sitting on a stool in the middle of our kitchen while Linda's scissors made clipping and clucking noises behind my back.

For the *next* twenty-three years and long thereafter until the present era of now I have divided my hair on the left side, just above the scar that runs from approximately my eyebrow up to the parting. I know that our children have always wondered why I part my hair on the left, and now the secret is told. It feels good to have gotten it out in the open, let me tell you.

So. What was it about those people we got to know in southern Utah? I don't know. The term "provincial" was very popular in the sixties and frequently mentioned in Cedar City, particularly by returned missionaries and others who had seen the Real World outside of Utah. Out there in that Real World we had peaceniks spouting brotherhood while plotting to exclude their neighbors from their atomic bomb shelters when the Russians pushed the button, politicians announcing they had no plans to bomb Cambodia (unless some of the planes sent to blow up Laos happened to stray across the border), people of both sexes threatening to give up their U.S. citizenship if they were forced to share a damn bus with them damn Negroes because this is the land of the free, dammit, and you can't tell them who to sit with. In the Real World, "better living through chemistry" referred to napalm, LSD, and vinyl clothing. In the Real World people could drive drunk through Smokey the Bear's national forests, throwing burning cigarettes out of the car window without giving it a second thought, while down in poor ol' provincial southern Utah the wiser of the elders were suggesting that hooch, nicotine, and fallout from the nearby atomic tests might be bad for the health of the community. Silly buggers.

What did they know? Meanwhile, we went on teaching, socializing, and playing in the desert like the provincials we really were.

7

"Everybody Knows"

Be determined in one mind and in one heart, united in all things.
2 Nephi 1:21

I've been debating whether to tell the following story. But now you *know* it's the following story so you already know I lost the debate. Some big air of mystery, huh?

Remember that I was young at the time, very young. Young faculty members tend to be the capering and gamboling lambs of the professorial herd, skipping around with enthusiasm and butting heads just because it's fun. Back in those days there were plenty of causes to be found. Everywhere. Our government had just passed a law that blacks were to be accorded equal treatment with whites, meaning that they could eat in the same places, drink from the same water fountains, and even pee into the same toilets. Young faculty took up the cause by encouraging students to ferret out local abuses of the new racial equality law. Women's rights were getting a toehold in the American consciousness, or if you weren't interested in sexism, you could turn hawk or dove concerning Vietnam. It was just a natural way of life to be ever on the alert for something to cure, kill, adopt, or protest about.

As faculty newspaper advisor, it sometimes made my life hell. Come to think of it, it did that every Thursday, the day I had to review the Friday edition. The student editor had a motto above his desk: "The job of a newspaper is to print the truth and raise hell." He also had a poster that said "To avoid criticism, say nothing, do nothing, be nothing."

So, he had me extrasensitized to the idea of social wrongs when the *Moby Dick* affair began.

As an undergrad I had taken an entire two-credit course in Melville's *Moby Dick.* I wrote two or three papers about the novel's symbolism, and I was impressed with the fact that my favorite intellectual, Bob Zoellner, had written a mighty tome about it, a book so erudite and obscure that almost no one could read it. Wow.

At Cedar City I was allowed to choose my own outside reading list for the introduction to literature course, and naturally I put *Moby Dick* on the list. Not because I thought the students would like it, although I knew some would; it was there because it was one of the few books I could expound upon. (English teachers, you know, have not read every book you ever heard of. One of our mottoes is "Read it? Heck, I haven't even *taught* it yet!")

Let us dub this young freshman "Joe" because it's a nice likable name. Like 80 percent of CSUtah's students, Joe was a local lad from Cedar City (the remainder came from such faraway Utah villages as mysterious American Fork, sanctified St. George, and scenic Enoch). Joe's family owned a small sundries shop where one might buy stationery, floral arrangements, small gifts, and inspirational literature.

I had arranged a meeting of all the students who had chosen *Moby Dick*, and we sat down around my conference table to discuss the intricacies of the interwoven symbolism. I began with the strange painting that Ishmael sees in the dimly lit tavern.

"With the ship in the painting being a schooner, and the hull unseen below the swell of ocean, the masts resemble the three crosses on Calvary. Comments?"

There were a few, but Joe looked puzzled.

"When the whalers suspend two whales on either side of the *Pequod*, Melville begins talking about philosophers Hume and Hobbes. Any idea why?"

Joe looked even more puzzled.

"Let's just play around with this idea of the *Pequod* being a microcosm. How does that notion affect the way you see the whale chase—especially if the whale represents malevolent evil to Ahab?"

Joe paged frantically through his book, which is when I noticed it was thinner than those of the other students. And heavily illustrated. I asked him to stay after our session and show it to me. And he did so, proudly. He had been given the book for Christmas.

"But it doesn't have all that symbol stuff in it," he said. "It's about a whale hunt. Big white whale."

I asked about his other favorite books. When I asked any question about our other readings in introduction to literature, he went blank. I pushed my copy of *Moby Dick* toward him and asked him to read a paragraph to me. Out of a hundred words or so, he recognized perhaps ten. Joe had a reading problem and—this was verified by the campus psychology professor after a series of tests—his mind had apparently ceased to develop at around age twelve.

My first reaction was to assume the role of Great Discoverer; I went into Chairman Rowley's office with my evidence and proudly announced that I had found a student who was enrolled in college but who could not read even the basic high school texts.

"I know," the chairman said. "But we don't have entrance requirements for Utah residents, other than graduating from an accredited Utah secondary school."

In the following week I went from Great Discoverer to Victim's Advocate. How had this happened? I started with the professor who taught our English education classes and who knew all about teaching certification for secondary teachers.

"Joe? Sure. Awfully nice kid. Everybody knows his family. Everybody likes him. And everybody including his classmates knows about his problem. Teachers usually gave him 'special' tests so he could get through school and graduate with the rest of his class."

Now I was the Indignant Professional From Outside This Provincial Backwater.

"But this is a college! He can't coast through here! I can't pass him. I can't give any kind of college credit to somebody who can't read at a college level! And that's just English. What about math, chemistry, history? If he gets into those classes and realizes why he's not seeing what the other students see, it will destroy him!"

"Well, we all like Joe. And he likes you too. He told me so. He said he might even major in English in a couple of years."

Small towns. No wonder it's a backwater. College is about competition for grades. It's a dog-eat-pup world, a meat grinder of battling intellects, a place where professors throw the innocent into the lion pit. So I shifted gears and became Excellent Counselor, Wise Advisor. I took out a composition assignment that I had once devised and made the class write it—because I wanted Joe's answer.

The essay question was, What Would You Really Rather Be Doing?

Students had confessed, in earlier engagements with this profound issue, that they would really rather be on fishing boats off Alaska, building surfboards on a Hawaiian beach, farming, working as loggers, designing dresses. One co-ed wrote that she wanted nothing more than to spend her life working in a chocolate factory, while another one said she'd like to try being a stripper for a couple of years and then go back to college.

Joe was blunt with me. In very simple sentences shot through with spelling errors and containing no punctuation other than an occasional period—some misplaced—he said he found college confusing. It was like being in a kind of fog where he could hear other people but couldn't make out what they were saying. Most of his books either didn't have pictures or they had pictures that didn't make any sense to him. What he really would like to do, he said, was to work in his parents' store. He liked running the cash register; they had a new one that told him how much change to give. He knew how to stock shelves and how to sort out the boxes in the storeroom. Most of all, he liked everyone who came in and they liked him.

I persuaded the psychologist to arrange a meeting with Joe's parents.

"I'm an outsider," I admitted. "I'm slowly finding out how things operate around here, and it's probably none of my business . . . "

And I laid out what I had "discovered" and how I felt about it. When I was finished, Joe's parents told me that neither of them had finished college and that Joe had gone to CSUtah simply because he wanted to be with his friends. To him it was just another year of high school.

"You're right," they agreed. "Some kids, they just aren't cut out for college. They don't need it for what they want to do, they don't like it, and they shouldn't have to do it."

"But like I said, I'm an outsider. I can't decide these things. It's not my business."

"Yes, it is. Dr. Braithwaite brought you here and we know he has good reasons for what he does. He brought you here to help the college go to a four-year school. You've got two college degrees and you're a professor. So you know what's what."

I almost said, "I'm not a professor. I'm only an instructor," meaning that my opinions carried very little weight.

Joe and I had another chat about his essay. I pointed out corrections he needed to make and he nodded his head. But he wasn't really getting it. I finally came right out and told him he wasn't going to get any happier in college. I suggested he go to work in his parents' store and stick with it until maybe finding something he would like even better. But not college.

Never before had I told a student to quit thinking of a college degree. Never since the day we left Utah have I seen Joe. What kind of life has he had? Did he find himself a nice wife? Does he have kids and grandkids by now? All these years and I still feel a pang of uncertainty when I think about Joe. What did I do to him, and what gave me the right?

Forty-five years later (from my journal):

Went to a middle school spring concert last night. One of our grandsons is a drummer in the band.

I was sitting in the bleachers remembering my own days in middle school musical evenings and how uncomfortable they were. I was a skinny little guy sitting with my arms wrapped around a big baritone horn, trying to keep my sweaty hands from losing their grip on the slick brass while peeking over at the other horns to see which valves I should be pushing down. Or I'd be in the school choir, balancing on the back row of risers and hoping the fat girl in front of me wouldn't crowd me off backward. Somebody next to me would usually make a joke and start the whole bass section giggling and getting scowls from Mr. Stowe, or else I would accidentally make eye contact with my mother and she'd wave at me. Concerts were only an hour long, but after fifty minutes I would look up at the clock and discover that only five minutes had actually passed.

At last night's middle school performance there was a young man shorter than his companions. He was in the choir. During not just one but two songs he had to step forward to the microphone and sing five or ten bars solo. Let's not hedge words here:

he sang flat. I'm no expert on music and I don't have perfect pitch, but even I could tell that this little guy had taken his pitch from the cracks between the black and white keys.

"I felt sorry for the little soloist," Sharon said as we walked toward the car afterward.

"Oh, boy!" I said. I could relate. When I was his age, you couldn't have gotten me to sing into a microphone even if you held a gun to my head. I knew I couldn't sing a lick. My friends knew it. If I tried it, I know what would have happened: my close buddies would tease me for the next two years; my parents would have suggested I take up some extracurricular activity other than music, such as wrestling or chess; and the girl who had *not* been allowed to sing a solo because Mr. Stowe wanted to give me a chance at it would organize all eight females in our school to boycott me until graduation.

Last night, however, I saw the middle school chorus reward the small soloist with high fives. I saw girls and boys alike patting his shoulder and giving him smiles. Sure, he had been nervous and even embarrassed, but his fellow choir members understood all about it.

I came away with that on my mind and thinking of Joe, all those years ago in Cedar City. It dawned on me, you see, why I didn't need to worry. Chairman Rowley had given me the reason and I hadn't seen it.

"Everybody knows about his problem."

I wasn't responsible for Joe's future. He had a whole community to take responsibility for his happiness. If he wanted to be in school, they would see to it. If he wanted to work in a store, they would make him feel good about himself doing it. That's what I saw, in microcosm, in the middle school concert last night. The world seems full of polarities and egotism, me-firsters and look-at-mes—but once in a while you see a bit of real community in action, and it restores your faith.

8

Don't Shoot the Gentile

But Ammon stood forth and began to cast stones at them with his sling; yea, with mighty power he did sling stones amongst them; and thus he slew a certain number.
Alma 17:36

Hard to believe, but back in the sixties you could get out of your car just about anywhere west of Cedar City and shoot tin cans, rocks, pine cones, and dangerous-looking tree stumps until your ammo ran out. Much of the land was unfenced. Primitive roads made a spider web in among the cedars and piñons and scrub oak. Some of the land was no doubt private, but you seldom saw a discouraging sign to that effect. Some of it was U.S. Forest Service land and everyone knew that USFS rangers had no authority to arrest you for shooting their stumps (if you were in violation of hunting regulations, they had to go hunt up a game warden or sheriff to hand you the ticket). The rest belonged to the BLM, which back then was the second biggest joke agency in the government, their reputation for nonaction and ineffectiveness running just slightly behind that of the BIA. There was even a local anecdote to explain it: on his way north to the Little Big Horn, Custer stopped off at the BIA and the BLM and told both agencies, "Don't do anything until I get back."

To me it was perfectly natural to grab the ol' Winchester .22 and a box of shells and head out for an afternoon's plinking. Back in Estes Park my boyhood buddies and I would do it on a weekly basis, shooting all over Prospect Mountain or riding our bikes out to Dry Gulch to assassinate gophers. Ranchers and stable owners welcomed us because we helped minimize the number of rodent holes in their pastures.

Owning a gun was as natural as having sneakers and a baseball hat. I remember one episode when I thought maybe my marriage might be in trouble because Sharon and I were talking about those "dates" we used to go on when I'd show her how to shoot. Not that either of us cared whether she could shoot or not; it was a good excuse to get my arms around her and show her how to keep the rifle steady. Then again, with my arms around her that front sight seemed to jump around like a grasshopper in a chicken pen.

"What kind of gun was that?" she asked me one evening.

What kind?

Here is a woman who can remember every hairstyle she has ever had (and those of her closest friends), who can tell you where and when she bought every pair of shoes in her two-closet collection of footwear, and who can remember the birth dates of not only our children but our grandchildren as well, and she can't recall a simple thing like a .22 Winchester Model 69A bolt action with five-shot clip, field peep sight, and military sling? Can I remain married to such a woman, no matter how good she is when it comes to necking?

That Winchester .22 rifle was, in fact, my first gun. My mother promised it to me if I joined the Estes Park Junior NRA Rifle Club and took gun safety lessons. The rifle club met on Wednesday nights outside of town in a long, dugout underground range heated by a single kerosene stove. We practiced on fifty-foot bull's-eye targets, five to a single sheet of paper. Within two years I worked my way up from pro-marksman and sharpshooter (with nine bars) to expert marksman.

No one paid much attention to permits or age in those days. Before I was out of high school I had owned a .22 pump Remington, a .32 H&R revolver, a 9-mm Mauser pocket pistol, a .32 Smith and Wesson, a 7.62-mm. Russian sniping rifle, a .410 double-barrel Chatham shotgun, and an antique single-shot .22 Savage vest pocket pistol. This little Savage inflicted the only accidental wound of any of my weapons, and it wasn't even me—the dumb kid up the road wanted to shoot it and closed the barrel with his hand over the muzzle and with the hammer all the way down. The .22 short slug made a neat round hole through his palm and out the back of his hand.

I bought the 7.62 sniping rifle because I thought I might like to do some elk hunting. But by the time I figured the cost of ammo, the cost of a license, and the cost of getting Doc Mall to reset my right shoulder every time I tried to sight in the 7.62, I might as well have spent the money on gasoline and driven around looking for fresh roadkill.

One thing I had hunted, besides gophers, was rabbits. My best pal, Jimmy Low, would get his Mossberg .22, I'd bring my Winchester, and we would become bunny hunters. Jimmy's mother would make us wait until after the first frost of autumn "to kill the bugs in their fur," but after that we could hardly wait to go hunting. These were cottontails, little brown rabbits that had two very fatal habits. When they saw a boy wearing a plaid hat with earflaps and carrying a .22 rifle, they would freeze and remain motionless while the selfsame boy rummaged his pockets for shells, dropped his mittens trying to fill the ammo clip, adjusted his glasses on his nose, braced himself in the official offhand shooting position sanctioned by the NRA, and squeezed off a lead pellet aimed at the eye because anywhere else it might spoil some meat.

The rabbit's other fateful habit was that it always ran in a circle. If we accidentally spooked one, it would take off at a hopping gallop, zigzagging among bushes and boulders in fear for its life. With good reason. We'd just look at each other and grin in our woodsmen way, knowing that if we only stood there in the snow with the wind solidifying the dribbles of snot from our noses long enough, the bunny would return. And if our fingers weren't frozen by then, we'd shoot him.

"Hey, Work!" Palmer said one Friday in Cedar City. "Wanna go out with us and shoot some jacks in the breaks tomorrow?"

"Jacks?"

For a moment I thought he meant Jack Mormons. These were Mormons who broke the rules and sometimes pretended not to belong to the Church. My imagination formed a Hitchcockian scenario in which a posse of guys in white cloaks and hoods went into the desert to seek and destroy Mormons accused of drinking or smoking or fudging on their tithings. And just to make it a nice mixed bag they were going to include a Colorado Gentile.

"Jackrabbits. There's millions of them out there."

"Oh! Jackrabbits!"

"What did you think I meant, Jack Mormons or something?"

"Never mind. Sure, count me in."

That evening I packed a lunch, oiled my boots, and put two boxes of shells in the pocket of my jeans jacket. Way too many cartridges for a few rabbits, but maybe some of the other guys would need to borrow some. As it turned out, I was underestimating the number of bullets I would need. By a factor of, say, two hundred.

Cedar breaks, oh best beloved, are groves or copses of fat, full, short trees growing in desert sand. There are these stubby cedar trees about the size of an SUV, then a bunch of stunted piñons. For her landscape accents Mother Nature also provides yucca plants and cacti. I was more used to hunting in ponderosa territory where bushes are not plentiful and you can see a long distance and where the odds of an animal being able to hide behind a tree are minimized.

So that's the jackrabbit venue. It reminded me of those arcade shooting galleries where little tin targets pop up behind an assortment of stumps, tree trunks, old tires, rusty oil drums, and abandoned cars. Come to think of it, parts of the cedar breaks looked exactly like that.

Before going further with this story I want to apologize to you four guys who took me on my first jackrabbit hunt. When I put my little Winchester .22 in the gun rack and climbed into one of the pickups, you were smiling sympathetically. I figured you just felt sorry for a guy who was so new in town that he didn't have anywhere to go and fire off a few hundred rounds of ammunition. Or maybe it was the same look that shopkeepers gave me when they learned I was a You-Know-What. Poor fellow, their expressions seemed to say. Condemned to a life of Pepsi and *Playboy* magazines. What a wretched existence.

It was my turn to smile in generous sympathy when we arrived at the cedar breaks and got out of the trucks. The other four took out their guns and started loading. Unfortunate provincials, I thought as I thumbed five .22 hollow points into my Winchester's clip. Either they can't afford a fine, accurate small bore like mine or they've never had the advantage of NRA marksmanship training. Have to use shotguns, for cripe's sake.

It was true. Bill broke open his 12-gauge and inserted a pair of #3 buckshot shells.

"Sporting goods store closed this morning, was it?" I inquired mirthfully.

"Why?"

"Well . . . number-three buck? I thought we was after rabbit. What do they do, charge when they're wounded?"

"Ha, ha."

Larry had removed the magazine plug on an expensive-looking Ithaca 12-gauge automatic and was loading up with #6 shot shells.

"Expecting to see some ducks, are we?" I laughed. "You guys. What's Irvin carrying today, a ten-gauge with double-ought buckshot? Ha, ha, ha!"

Irvin cast a glance at my little .22 and held out his gun for me to look at. It was a 16-gauge pump with a choke on the barrel that looked like somebody had taken his gun and welded onto it the muffler from a 1941 John Deere.

"I've just got number-six shot," he said apologetically, "but with this choke I can get 'er out there about a hundred fifty yards."

As for Palmer, he came staggering under the weight of an antique Greener that he proudly showed me.

"This shotgun came across the prairies in a Mormon pioneer handcart," he said.

I doubted it, mostly because almost anything rusty in Utah is said to have arrived on handcarts all the way from Illinois, Ohio, or even Bulgaria. The floor lamp we bought at a garage sale had come by handcart. Come to think of it, the lady said the garage had also come across the prairies on a handcart.

"So you're the double-ought buckshot guy, I guess." I chortled. "I'll bet you're going to bring up the rear in case any jackrabbits try to sneak up behind us with clubs."

"Store was still closed this morning," Palmer said. "I'll have to make do with number-three buckshot."

Time for a firepower inventory. One guy was carrying a shotgun so tightly choked that it could cut a good-sized piñon tree in half and kill the bunny behind it. Another was packing a semiautomatic shotgun that could project a wall of lead shot even a mosquito couldn't penetrate—each BB of his #6 shot was only half the size of one of my .22 rounds, and he had the advantage of being able to keep a hundred BBs in the air at a time.

As for the other two shotgunners in our party, at the first sight of movement they were prepared to pepper the landscape with lead balls measuring a quarter inch in diameter, or .03 larger than my .22 slugs.

"I guess we're not out here for meat, then," I said, snickering and guffawing. "Just the 'sportsmanship' of shooting, ha, ha, ha."

Indeed, any creature smaller than a Cape buffalo that might stumble into our line of fire would be reduced to hash rendered unfit for human consumption by a dangerous additive, namely half a pound of lead per pound of hamburger.

So away we went, me and Irvin on the left flank while Bill, Larry, and Palmer spread out to our right. We hadn't walked more than two minutes before we heard Bill cry out, "Jack!" In the same instant we felt the concussion of a 12-gauge and saw sand, dust, and assorted parts of piñon trees flying off toward Nevada.

"Bill missed! You take 'im!" Irvin yelled.

There was a flash of movement off to the right twenty yards ahead of me. I shouldered my .22 and sighted through the rear peep.

It might have been a jackrabbit that went streaking through my peep sight, but I can't be sure. Something gray came from behind a tree and vanished behind the next one. It seemed to have legs that whirred around in a blur like the roadrunner in those cartoons.

"You didn't shoot," Irvin observed.

"Ah. Yes. Well . . . that was a doe. Back in Colorado we only shoot the bucks."

"Jack!" came a cry from Palmer, followed by a blast that was either his 10-gauge or the reopening of hostilities at the Alamo. Larry pumped off three shots at the unfortunate hare. If you go out there today, you can probably still see the arroyo his shotgun pellets created. Then Irvin offered me the next chance.

This time I saw the gray streak coming. I gave him a hundred-yard lead and squeezed off my shot.

"Pop!" went my gun, and before I could open the bolt to chamber another deadly .22 long-rifle hollow point, the jackrabbit was hiding behind a trash can somewhere in downtown St. George.

"What was that all about?" Irvin asked. "You missed him, huh?"

"Heck no. I've seen this happen back in Colorado," I explained. "Sometimes a rabbit or even a duck is so scared that their adrenalin keeps them moving after they've been hit. They don't know that they're still running even though I just shot a bullet through their little heart. They keep running or flying until they drop somewhere, and you never can find them afterward, even with a dog."

"Pathetic," Irvin said.

"Isn't it?" I agreed. "Poor animals."

"I didn't mean the animals."

We hunted until late afternoon, and "hunted" is the word for it. Good thing our five-man tribe of hunter-gatherers knew where to find a grocery store. I got off two more shots during the next three hours—one because I thought a gray cedar stump was a sitting jackrabbit and one because a little dust devil came whirlwinding toward me and I took it for an attacking jack.

Among the five of us we pretty much killed eighteen yucca, sixteen large cacti, and several innocent saplings. Palmer insisted on demonstrating the power of his 10-gauge by shooting at an old five-gallon can, and we all admitted that it was an impressive sight to see shredded metal falling on the piñons and making them look like kids had been throwing the Christmas tinsel.

We stopped to eat lunch, giving our ears a chance to recover from the bombardment of shotgun blasts—and the "pop!" of my .22—and when the ringing in my head more or less ceased (was that the doorbell?), I heard a strange, low, inhuman sound coming from the sage. My first thought was that it was aliens from a flying saucer—people were beginning to see them in New Mexico.

"Aliens, you think?" I said.

"Nah," Palmer replied, holding his sandwich in his mouth while he brought his 10-gauge shotgun to his shoulder and fired a couple of pounds of #3 shot in the general direction of the noise.

"It's the damn jackrabbits," he said. "They like t' sit out there and laugh at us."

Palmer voted for going home, since he had to go to campus the next day and take care of some emergency at the physical plant where he worked. But the rest of us being faculty and therefore pretty much at loose ends overruled him and decided we'd make one more sweep through the cedar breaks. I was all for it, not because I harbored any hope of hitting a running jackrabbit with a .22 and thus earning myself a place in the record books as the only person to have ever done so, but because during our morning exercise I had picked up a piece of flint arrowhead and a pottery shard. If we did another sweep, I might find other artifacts under the litter of pulverized pine needles and expended lead shot.

An ancient Ute Indian probably saved my life that day. The Utes once roamed the region—hence the name Utah—so perhaps my savior was a Ute warrior. Maybe he was out in the cedar breaks one day and shot an arrow at a jackrabbit, only to shatter his flint arrowhead on a rock instead.

"Stop laughing, Stewmeat!" screamed the ancient Ute as he threw away the broken arrow point and ran after the offending hare, his stone knife flashing in the Utah sun.

The same moment that I saw the broken arrowhead and knelt down to pick it up I heard the dreaded cry "*Jack!*" ring out through the trees, and I was about to answer by yelling, "*So what?*" when something very fast and very solid went roaring through the tree branches above me. It may have been one of the F-3 jet fighters that sometimes made low-level practice runs in the desert, except they don't usually cause a deluge of falling pine needles and cones. Nonetheless, I turned to see if a jet would rise up into a banking climb at the edge of the cedar breaks—but all I saw was Irvin running toward me. He was looking at his 16-gauge, full-choked shotgun as if trying to figure out why he had missed me.

Larry came hurrying toward me from the other direction.

"Damn, Irv!" Larry said. "Don't shoot the Gentile, or we'll have to hire another one!"

"But he looked like a jackrabbit all scrunched down like that. Or a coyote."

"I'm wearing a red jacket," I pointed out.

"Foxes are red, sometimes."

"I want to go home."

"Bear, maybe. I've heard bears sometimes come down from the mountains."

"Wearing red jackets? Let's just forget it, Irvin. It was just a bad shot."

"Well, you shot a stump."

"What did Larry mean, 'We'll have to hire another one'?" I asked.

"Did I say that?" Larry asked, all innocent-like. "Just kidding. What I meant to say was don't shoot the Gentile, he's doing the best he can."

9

A Fine and Private Desert

. . . in this the beginning of the rising up and the coming forth of my church out of the wilderness.

Doctrine and Covenants 5:14

I've already broached the subjects of desert wilderness and macho men who like to look in the mirror and see themselves hunter-gatherers, so I may as well proceed in the same vein.

I'm immediately impaled upon the horns of a dilemma. In the spirit of my CSUtah colleague Harry Plummer, I'm tempted to begin with a thoroughgoing etymology and definition of the word "desert"; however, in my long illustrious career as a writin' teechur I have strenuously opposed the plebian habit of starting speeches and essays with that worn-out and obnoxious phrase "according to Webster's dictionary . . . "

No offense intended, but a dictionary definition is a stupid way to begin. First of all, the term being defined is usually one that does not need definition, so you're saying to your audience, "Hey, idiots, you're not smart enough to know what 'wilderness' means so I looked it up for you." Either that or you're saying, "Hey, lamebrains, you aren't even bright enough to look it up for yourself."

You're also saying, "I'm not creative enough to definate it in my own words, so I'm going to quotate it from the dictionary where I had to researchicate it myself."

Great opening.

My other gripe about this trite, clichéd, and hackneyed way of getting into your topic is the use of the phrase "according to Webster's dictionary" when you are actually quoting a New Collegiate or an American Heritage or an Oxford English dictionary. This tells the reader that you don't know that "Webster" is not a generic term for dictionaries any more than "Ford" is a generic term for anything that has four wheels and needs frequent repair.

On the other hand, when I went looking for the etymology of this term "desert," I was reminded of an interesting connection between the noun and the verb. Desert (the noun) means "any place where a breeze leaves grit in your socks and the humidity is so low that picking your nose could make you bleed to death." Desert (the verb) means "to abandon, leave, depart from, ignore henceforth, exile, or say 'wait right here for me' with no intention of returning." When the early Europeans decided to desert the thirteen colonies and head toward the sunset, they came to an open treeless sea of grass they dubbed the Great American Desert.

Which leads to the connection between desert places and mythology. To a stuffy scholar such as myself, "myth" is a term meaning a story that defines or identifies a particular culture. Presbyterians, for example, reject the mythology of transubstantiation while embracing the mythology of grace. "Myth" in this context does not mean "unreal" or "fantastic" such as a Presbyterian church with a balanced budget and no building program.

One well-known piece of mythology is the record of a man who led his people into the desert, communicated with God, provided water and food, and was given divine insight. I refer, of course, to Charlton Heston, one of the most macho guys who ever pulled a trigger. He also drove a mean chariot, but that's a different story.

Charlton Heston spent a great deal of time in the land of sand, but for me, living in Cedar City was my first experience with the desert. Up until then I had known only the high Colorado mountains with their crystal streams and green meadows, and my only brush with anything like arid land was when my father took us to visit his birthplace in eastern Colorado, out where a stream aptly named the Platte oozed through the silt and among the tumbleweeds and cactus.

On our weekend excursions out of Cedar City we discovered the magic of dunes where the girls and the dog could play in wonderland drifts of barefoot-warm sand. We found secret springs and hidden seeps of water beneath shaded cliffs where watercress, duckweed, and thick grass held back the wind-driven sand. Under cedars and piñon trees and especially on those hillslopes facing the warm morning sun after a windy night we found broken arrowheads, flint scrapers, and potshards. It was in the desert that we found our little dingo-looking dog that we named "Sandy" partly because she was the color of the dunes and partly because wherever she stood or sat in the house she would leave a little pile of sand behind. So did the two daughters, come to think about it, but they already had names.

Some say that the Mormon pioneers chose to settle in Utah's desert because Brigham Young rose up and looked down on the valley (like Charlton Heston gazing out from the top of Mount Pisgah in *Exodus*, but that's another story) and said, "This here's the spot," which was changed to "this is the place" as soon as the state could afford English professors. Another theory is that the beleaguered Mormons moved away from Illinois—a *long* ways away—because of disagreements with Nauvoo's neighborhood planning committee and vowed not to stop until they found a spot where their only neighbors would be venomous crawly things.

Me? I think they settled in Utah because of mythology. Mythology and the problem of Mormon malehood. In Cedar City I heard numerous stories about pioneers and Mormon men. I heard them anytime someone in the creative writing class read us an essay about their ancestors, which was pretty much every Wednesday night. I routinely tried to suggest that they write about something equally Mormon such as the irrigation systems in Cedar City's streets or family recipes for Jell-O, but I'd get the Mormon Male Pioneer diced up and served to me instead.

Joseph Smith, the finder of the tablets and the founder of the Church, was the one who started it all. He had the revelation from God but unfortunately it happened in New York State where there were too many trees. According to humankind's general mythology, religions do not begin in forested, fertile places like New York. They start in deserts. When was the last time you heard of a major religion beginning in a jungle, for instance?

Or the Arctic. Ever hear of Eskimos or Inuits starting a major religion that spread across the world? Even the Baptists can't get a foothold in the Arctic, possibly because of that baptism-by-total-immersion idea.

Deserts. That's where your philosophers and holy men come from. Even astronomers and astrologers, like the ancient Chaldeans who virtually discovered astronomy. It's just part of the scheme: if you're going to be a major religion founder like Jesus or Charlton, you need to go out into a desert ("place where negative water supply discourages plant growth") where you feel like the Big Power has deserted you ("left alone, abandoned, told to shove off"), and *there* you get the insight and inspiration. A desert also makes a dandy place in which to put your faith through some serious and sincere testing. Why else were Adam and Eve tossed into a wasteland if not to see whether their faith would hold up? It's hard to have your faith tested while you're eating grapes and apricots and gentle breezes are wafting over your body as you lie on a couch of fragrant herbage.

You can also see a long way in a desert. You can see so far that people sometimes see things that don't even exist, like mirages, UFOs, and dependable used cars. And because humankind is the philosophical animal, the only animal (apparently) capable of abstract thought, we are always being driven to see connections. Like the metaphoric metamorphosis when we take "I can see purty far" and transmute it into "I'm a far-seeing son-of-a-gun, symbolically speaking." Out in a desert where there's lots of light and distance we just naturally experience lots of mental enlightenment and distancing from the body. (See "Chaldeans," above.)

Looking at history, the situation seems pretty obvious: whenever a new mythology comes along, especially if it includes revelations, prophecies, vision quests, dire warnings, and divine beings, you need to hunt yourself up a good desert to really maximize the experience. Forming a mythology system in downtown Los Angeles or a retirement village near Miami simply isn't going to work.

The trouble comes when your desert-bound people decide they're getting tired of living in goatskin tents and drinking out of cacti. At that point somebody inevitably comes up with the idea of Adapting. Not adapting people to fit whatever environment they find themselves in—leave that for the piñon trees and yucca plants to figure out. Nossir, you are a human and therefore your life is governed by a desperate desire to adapt the environment to fit your needs. If you find your carriage wheels sinking into the sand, you pave paths and call them streets. Slam a dam across a valley or two, dig a ditch here and there, and you can have flush toilets. Then electricity comes along and POW! Bingo halls, slot machines, movie theaters, and before you know it, you got big trouble, right here in River City.

Cities become the problem. Ever hear of the Almighty punishing people in the wilderness? Oh, sure, a bad case of boils here and there, possibly a serpent attack. But for real Almighty retribution you need to look to the cities. Look what happened to Sodom. To Gomorrah. To Babylon, for crying out loud. I'm even thinking that maybe Pompeii had it coming. When I'm approaching Las Vegas, I put the accelerator to the floorboards and keep going.

So what about the men mentioned earlier, you are asking. That part of the story goes like this: a movement toward the Latter-day interpretation of the Word of God began with a single man in 1823. Within ten years it was the Church of Jesus Christ, but the leaders and their followers were still wandering around in the "wilderness" of New York (no doubt deluded by James Fenimore Cooper's romance novels into believing that the American frontier was somewhere along the banks of the Ohio River). Persecution began, misunderstanding flourished, and the Latter-day Saints joined the stream of Americans heading for free land and opportunity west of the Missouri.

And on a related topic, take an overview of western European civilization from the end of the Dark Ages until the Enlightened Atomic Age and you'll see that there's a difference between males and females.

Throughout the centuries, females have been judged according to "keep." As in "she sure keeps those kids clean," "she keeps a good house," "she keeps 'em in school," "she keeps the kids at their homework," "she keeps after her old man, all right," and "ask her who Grampa Roberts was, she keeps the family Bible." She also keeps the photo albums, the heirloom linens, crystal, silver, and family recipes. She keeps the piano tuned, keeps the budget, keeps herself lookin' good, keeps on going when things get rough, and keeps up with current events.

The neighborhood might also judge her by what she doesn't keep. She can't seem to keep any money. Can't keep that car running. Can't keep those kids in shoes. Or she lost something—lost her zest for life, lost her home, lost her husband, lost her mind. Tsk tsk.

Pick up a group of persons, toss them into the desert to sink or swim, and keeping becomes not just important but essential.

The family record needs to be kept, the kids need to be kept at their book learnin', food needs to be brought in and kept for the winter, clothes have to be kept in repair. So the women who do it best become valued most highly. And here's the unfortunate thing: being a good keeper becomes society's standard by which anyone in the female persuasion is judged, even those women who don't give a fig about "keeping," house or otherwise.

During the decade I'm talking about some women became *really* angry about all this. So angry that they took it out on clothing, food, and hairdos. Believe it or not, they took to eating stuff like tofu and yogurt, cut their hair short or let it hang long from ugly headbands, tied their shirts into knots and dyed them in psychedelic patterns, and immolated brassieres by public incineration (after removing them, of course).

The male animal of the *homo sap* species, on the other hand, is measured according to "get," not "keep." What kind of guy is he? He gets along with his neighbors. He gets a good salary. He gets going when the going gets tough. He's getting up in the world. He gets the Big Picture. His sense of humor really gets me. He gets respect, by golly. When they go out to eat, he gets the check.

A man gets back at those who mess with him. He gets around his boss, the cops, the neighborhood covenants, and the IRS. He gets away with murder (figuratively speaking). He's getting by, by gosh. Gets along OK, if you know what I mean. We like the way he gets about—just last month he managed to get away for a little vacation. In fact, he's planning to build a getaway cabin up on Iron Creek or on the Kolob Plateau or somewhere.

We like the way he gets out of doing things he doesn't like to do, but we get down on him if we think he's not getting anywhere. If he has a business and it's getting nowhere, he's a loser. And we would tell him what he's doing wrong, if we thought we could get through to him.

Back in the 1800s when the persecution became unbearable, the Latter-day Saints needed to find a state or territory that they could have to themselves, one where their Christian neighbors did not have a surplus of feathers and tar.

The Far West beckoned.

In answering the call, these attributes of the post-Dark Ages male came to the fore, or at least that's what the myth tells us. Real men, men of value, were those who got going, got themselves an outfit, got their family together, and got the hell across the Missouri. They went west in order to get things for their descendants—life, liberty, property—and a smart person wouldn't get in their way. What were needed were men who took charge, made decisions, got things organized. The women who supported them kept the family fed and clothed and kept their spirits up.

Such human traits as these tend to get ingrained. Ingrained and trotted out for exercise every once in a while. Distant ancestors in my own Celtic background had to wear long, heavy woolen blankets because they herded sheep in the drizzling cold Scottish highlands. They carried knives to eat half-cooked mutton and hack their way into the Scottish geologic phenomena known as "bannock," a kind of man-made rock created from oat flour scorched over a peat fire.

And to this very day, every once in a while a bunch of guys nicknamed Mac meet someplace where they can dress up in skirts with blankets wrapped around their shoulders, throw telephone poles at each other, and limp around because they have little knives in their socks. Mythology is a powerful and sometimes peculiar thing.

In Cedar City we encountered one or two males who held fast to the belief that a Real Man was the boss of his wife and the one who made decisions for the neighborhood, parish, ward, or state. They seemed to believe that they were still living back in the days of the ancient Hebrews when the marauding Gentiles could show up at the city walls. And if it happened here in our own time, they implied, all hell would break loose.

There we would be, suddenly called upon to sally forth and doeth horrid battle and layeth waste to Jehovah's enemies. And who, they asked, would you want to see in the forefront leading the troops? Charlton Heston, who not only had the backing of the NRA but could get water from rocks and who told the pharaoh to find himself another work force? Or would you rather have a bunch of women leading the charge? The women would no doubt want to "talk about it" first. Then the women would go around making sure that everybody was OK. And when the troops and chariots and horses were all assembled in rank and file and prepared to go forth from the city gates to engage the enemy, the women would say, "Now, does anyone need to go to the bathroom before we leave?"

One day we were in our backyard and heard crashing noises coming from the yard behind us. It sounded like crockery being smashed into a steel oil drum, the kind many people used for trash cans.

We investigated and discovered Abigail Conron, one of our neighbors, methodically hurling an entire set of china into the Conron trash drum one piece at a time. Soup bowl followed salad plate, saucer followed gravy boat, and all the while Abigail wore a smile that if could not be called "beatific," could at least be called "self-satisfied." Had she flipped? Had she gone 'round the bend? We knew that her husband, Abraham, could be a dictatorial, overbearing, autocratic irritant. He kept a very close eye on my garage, for instance. He told me how high to mow my grass. If I let the sprinkler run a quarter hour too long, he would be on the phone demanding to know why. He liked the fact that I walked to work, and I had seen him scowl at me if I drove the car.

Dogs went on Abraham's lawn only once. I'd believe you if you told me that the newspaper boy asked permission to walk up to his porch. Once, a telephone company repair truck was stolen in the night. The joyriders drove it into the desert where they got in a panic and set fire to it. Abraham wrote letters to the editor, interrogated the police force, searched the desert for clues, and I'm pretty sure organized a lynch party to deal with this offense against Cedar City society. And here was Abigail, mirthfully smashing the family dishes into the trash can.

"Hey, Abby!" we began.

"Oh, hi, Jim! Hi, Sharon! How are you two today?"

"Just fine. Nice day."

"Lovely. Just lovely."

"So," I said, grinning disarmingly as I peered into the oil drum at the shards, "are you tired of washing dishes or something?"

"Ha, ha! That's a good one! No, I'm just tired of this set of dishes. I mean really tired of them. Know what I mean?"

"Do I ever!" Sharon exclaimed. "Jim has this one necktie. I feel like I'm going to toss my cookies every time he puts it on."

"Bring it over and throw it in my trash barrel," Abigail offered. "You've no idea how good it can make you feel."

"So this is a kind of therapy, smashing plates?" I asked.

"Yes, but that's not why I'm doing it," she said. "I complained to Abraham the other day, and he said we would not buy new dishes until every last one of these had been broken."

She held up a large platter she'd been saving back and hurled it into the oil drum with a vengeance that reminded me of Victor Mature throwing that Philistine guy down the temple steps in the movie *Samson and Delilah*.

"And this place setting, I think," Abigail said merrily, "is the last one to be broken!"

Her spouse had forgotten, you see, that the community's need for headstrong dictatorial males had left town with the last handcart. So she countered by "forgetting" how she was supposed to keep stuff.

Abigail insisted that I try my hand at smashing a soup bowl. I have to admit it felt good, pitching porcelain against steel.

"Thanks," I said.

"No, thank *you*," she replied. "Now when Abraham asks me if I broke every one of the dishes, I can truthfully say that I didn't."

10

Teasing the Beehives and Bringing in the Sheathes

Is not the life more than meat, and the body than raiment?
3 Nephi 13:25

To paraphrase Mark Twain, I would be very much obliged to any gentleman who could explain to me if there is any logic in the design of human clothing. Beginning in puberty when I was an avid reader of any issue of *National Geographic* featuring unclad subequatorial females, I gradually became aware that people dress for their environment. Eskimos wear layers of sealskin and fur. Tahitians wear layers of mostly flowers. I once had a foreign graduate student, a Tuareg from the deserts of Libya, who told me that the black tents of the Tuaregs, like the voluminous robes they wore, were quite efficient at turning away the scorching heat. And I believed him. A Tuareg warrior wearing a Speedo would have a slim chance of survival.

I also grew up with the belief that there was a connection between applying fresh shoe polish to one's brogans and going to church. Church also meant putting on my white shirt and either my best patches pants or else my whistle-britches corduroy trousers. Men whom I saw all week wearing coveralls or Levi's would show up at church in blue serge suits with a five-dollar strip of cloth knotted around their necks. Women would change from café waitress uniforms or plaid shirts and jeans into skirts and nylon hosiery.

Christmas apparently required little boys to get decked out in their mother's old chenille bathrobe and stand on a stage holding a shepherd's crook while the town delinquent played Joseph and the snotty teacher's pet girl pretended to be Mary the Virgin. There was *some* connection, we knew, between the Bible, the Community Church of the Rockies, and bathrobes. We just didn't know what it was.

I was also to learn, years after *National Geographic* had ceased to be instructive, that clothing can also be a means females employ in order to entice males into mating. It turns out that the Bible has nothing to say on the subject of wearing spike heels and sheer hosiery into church, but a German guy named Sigmund Freud sure did. I doubt whether there's any connection between Utah, Mormonism, and fashions of the sixties, but it was in Utah in the sixties that I encountered three of the strangest clothing rituals ever known to humankind. I refer, of course, to the beehive hairdo, the sheath dress, and the panty girdle.

We had come from Fort Collins, one of the nation's cutting-edge centers for coiffure and fashion. Sure, people from Boulder poked fun at us for being an agricultural college ("Colorado's Udder University" and "Silo Tech" being among the nicknames they had for us), but you could bet that if a hairstyle or skirt length had showed up on *77 Sunset Strip*, *American Bandstand*, or *I Dream of Jeannie*, the CSU women would adopt it. Being urbane and sophisticated, it was natural that we should be amused by Cedar City where styles ran more toward reruns of *Petticoat Junction* and *Ozzie and Harriett.*

Nonetheless, the beehive became the official emblem of Utah in 1959. Utah women showed support by piling up their hair into the shape of a tall beehive, or in the case of a woman who wore bifocals, the shape of a camel's hump. This modish manner of wearing the hair would be best described by process. A more accomplished writer might find parallels between the struggles of a woman trying to force her hair into a beehive shape and the labors the Mormons faced in reaching Utah.

But I can't do that.

To begin, a woman had to allow her hair to attain shoulder length or better. Using a coarse-tooth comb not unlike one that might be used to curry a feral Rambouillet, she would drag each straggling strand to join others in straight lines running down her back, over her shoulders, and across her face. (Rumor had it that this is where the creators of the television show *The Addams Family* got the idea for Cousin It, but that's another story.)

Using various miniature hay rakes and hot irons, she would begin "teasing" the hair, causing it to fray and tangle and curl and twist. The mess would be tortured either to the right or to the left, depending upon one's style preference, until it gradually acquired the appearance of a big ball of cotton candy sitting atop her skull. Then the spraying would begin. Out would come a pressurized aerosol can of lacquer and soon the bedroom would be under a fog of spray that settled on all the flat surfaces in the place, including the window. After repeated episodes of creating a beehive hairdo, most bedroom windows became opaque enough to use in bathrooms and the bedspread could be stood on edge against a wall.

At this time a folk legend circulated. It seems that a stylish woman was teasing and piling and teasing and spraying lacquer on her hair inside a camping trailer while standing too close to a butane light fixture. Her husband was startled by a brilliant sudden glare like an old-fashioned flashbulb going off and turned to see his wife virtually bald and a black spot on the ceiling just above where her hair used to be.

Possibly the most comic thing about beehive hairdos was watching a lady as she tried to don something to protect her sculptural labors. No ordinary hat would come close to covering it, nor would an ordinary scarf. Nothing short of an army shelter half would do the job. Umbrella sales skyrocketed during the beehive decade.

You may be thinking, "Mock the ladies if you dare, Work, but what about you men with all of your silly facial growth and goofy hairstyles?"

Sorry to disappoint, but back in those days the wearing of beards was restricted by law to church elders, desert prophets, and, for those towns that had them, the town drunk. Each day every other male faced himself in the mirror, put a shiny new blue blade into his so-called safety razor, and applied cold sharp steel to his tender flesh. Some opted for the electric razor, which had evolved to the point where the buzzing blades ripped off only the top micron of skin as they yanked the whiskers out by the roots. A few brave souls bragged that they used an old-fashioned cutthroat razor, although not many of these had survived the straight-razor days.

After scraping off his overnight stubble, the stalwart fellow would splash his face with one of an assortment of liquids known as "lotion," a word that implies a soothing, nourishing kind of effect. But aftershave lotion, whether made by Bay Rum, Old Spice, English Leather, or SeaForth, consisted of one active ingredient: alcohol. Should you ever be curious as to the meaning of "active ingredient," scrape some part of your body until the flesh is red and then apply alcohol to it. It will render you active as all get-out, I guarantee.

What about men's hair? Some men allowed their wives to cut their hair, and in my case a neighbor who had consumed a quart of cheap wine. But most men paid a barber upward of a buck and a half for the privilege. The barber would make an elaborate show of settling you into his upholstered chair where he wrapped you in a drop cloth, secured a little paper collar around your neck, and asked one of two questions. The first was "how do y' want it?" and the second was "how about them Cubs?" and you might as well go ahead and talk about the Cubs because you were going to have your hair cut the way he wanted it anyway.

Clippers all the way 'round, sideburns cut even with the tops of your ears, and neck shaved. Up top he lifted your locks with his comb and scissored off anything longer than his pinkie finger.

Five minutes and you were finished. The barber would dust you with some sinus-clogging powder, unclasp the drop cloth, shake it so that your hair trimmings went down your pants and into your shoes, and wipe his comb and scissors on a damp towel.

"Next!"

As for men's fashion, the Cedar City professionals—car dealers, real estate salesmen, and professors—were still wearing the Ivy League suit when we arrived. And that suited me just fine since my clothing allowance was so meager. (By the time I had saved up enough pennies to buy myself a Nehru jacket, they had gone out of style.) Reckless in its antiestablishment statement, the Ivy League suit featured trousers with cuffs but without pleats or seams! This shocked our elders. They could remember being in the army and navy where knife-sharp creases were required on your pants, shirts, and underwear. To add to the shock we wore our collars buttoned down and boldly ventured forth without wearing any collar stays! And our coats were (gasp!) single breasted and had three buttons.

For semi-formal wear, meaning just about any time you left the house without carrying either garden implements or the garbage, women preferred the sheath. Sheath dress, sheath skirt. If you have ever carried something in a sheath, such as a hunting knife or a hand axe, you know that the primary requirement is that the sheath fit the thing so tightly that it won't fall out. I believe I'm safe in saying that no man ever saw a woman fall out of a sheath dress.

Spandex had been invented but was not yet being used for street wear. As far as I could determine by looking closely at a number of sheath-clad females (but not closely enough as to endanger my marriage), the material seemed to be a species of industrial strength linen or possibly silk. In some cases the material was being torture-tested to almost inhuman limits—and I didn't even want to think about the stress being placed on the human cells and tissue trapped inside that material.

For a desert people who presumably remembered walking across the continent to arrive at Utah and who presumably spent time on their knees thanking God for the experience, the sheath dressed seemed ridiculously inappropriate. Then again, maybe the women were being punished or doing penance for something and the stores didn't sell sackcloth and ashes.

A woman dressing herself in one of these unlikely costumes today would make a winning entry for *Funniest Home Videos*. Luckily, the only visual recording devices back then were hand-wound 8-mm cameras that not only required intense lighting but also required you to take them to the drugstore for developing. These two factors rather militated against husbands filming their wives in the act of dressing. Had the modern digital camera existed during the sheath dress fad, no doubt the nation would be littered with unmarked graves while the cocktail lounges would be full of well-tailored widows.

What follows is the process, as told to me by a group of male informants who wish to remain anonymous but with whom I play poker twice a month.

It began with one bare lady and a large economy-size can of talcum powder that was liberally dusted over the area to be covered. This was *not* for hygienic or attractant purposes: it was for lubrication. The lady held aloft the first piece of apparel, a device apparently invented by the Spanish Inquisition and sold under the innocuous-sounding label "panty girdle." The observing males assured me that in its out-of-the-packaging state the panty girdle looked small enough to serve as an elbow brace.

She now sat down and to the astonishment of her husband actually began tugging and forcing the elasticized tube over her feet. With more tugging and pulling and powdering she managed to get it up over her calves and stand up. She now resembled a flesh-colored light bulb about to enter a nudist sack race.

One thing about it: the panty girdle kept a woman's arms in great shape. Up and up she heaved and towed it, the rubber screeching inside the fabric, seams straining as one industrial-strength elastic strand was compressed against another. The waistband reached the overhang where all hands were called to the rear to haul away. Time was of the essence; she had been holding her breath ever since the tiny tube was around her knees and her oxygen was about to run out.

Finally, with a great sigh and inhalation of oxygen, she felt the waistband snugging her waist and smiled at her accomplishment. No man, not even one of those football players who wear stretchy underwear, could hope to achieve the feat of compressing an adult body into a garment intended for a Barbie doll. She looked trim; she looked fit. She could almost breathe. She was about ready to don the outer sheath. All she needed was to put on her bra with its hardened linen cups sewn into points with nylon cord and her warm "slip" garment, for which I surmise was either to prevent frostbite inside the sheath or prevent inquiring eyes from seeing through the panty girdle. Then came her stockings.

The stockings. After the Iron Maiden panty girdle, the stockings were incredibly thin, frail things that would "run" at the slightest touch. I am told that some women actually wore white cotton gloves in order to put on these stockings so as not to ruin them. Stockings, as I understand it, are worn inside shoes to provide warmth and protection from blisters. Sheer nylon stockings make little or no sense in this context.

The stockings were held up by means of a set of clasps hidden beneath the lower edge of the panty girdle. I'll say no more about it, except to say that Boy Scouts could use those clasps to secure a tarp in a hurricane.

The sheath enclosed the under-paraphernalia like a sausage skin—a sausage skin made of material thick enough to conceal the contours of clasps, hooks, and buttons. Once the zipper of this sheath had been closed all the way from derrière to neck, and sometimes from waist to armpit as well, the damsel was more or less impervious to harm. The garment enforced excellent vertical posture and had an undeniable slimming effect. An assembly of women in sheath dresses and beehive hairdos resembled a box of cotton swabs.

Looking back, I realize that my habit of wearing tie and jacket to class began there in southern Utah and stayed with me throughout my career, even when colleagues could be found teaching class in cutoff shorts and T-shirts. I never could do that, partly because the sight of my skinny white legs is enough to send storks into gales of helpless mirth and partly because that little college at the edge of the desert imprinted me with a sense of the formality of things.

You can still witness this kind of formality, this sense of decorum, at a university graduation ceremony. It is an occasion ruled by forms. The shape of a bachelor's gown is one form. The master's gown has its own form, as does that of the PhD raiment. Even the colors have significance—the color of the hood lining and the color of trim on the robe tell you the scholar's school and field of study.

College itself is also a formal situation although many modern collegians seem to have forgotten it. Here is the professor; here is the student. Out of respect for his discipline and out of respect for his students, the professor wears "formal" attire. Out of respect for *their* position in the academic hierarchy, students should also wear some kind of formal or uniform garb.

Maybe it could be attributed to the fact that so many of Cedar City's residents attended church regularly, but that feeling of formality was there, a certain comforting feeling that everything was in its place and all was right with the world.

I stole the "all was right with the world" line from Robert Browning because it makes a dandy segue into the next chapter.

11

Returning

Once in a cycle the comet
Doubles its lonesome track.
Enriched with the tears of a thousand years,
Aeschylus wanders back.
John G. Neihardt, "The Poet's Town"

Two years passed and the Colorado mountains were calling us to come home. The Forest Service wrote to ask if I would be available for the summer fire crew again. At Colorado State University, my nemesis Rex Nostrum had finally removed himself from the college, leaving the English department in the care of two co-chairmen who offered me an instructorship. Our parents were missing the little granddaughters.

Time to decide. Time to seize the day, follow our bliss, or just close our eyes, count to three, and jump toward the future.

It had become pretty clear to me that if we were going to stay at CSUtah, I would need to figure out an academic long-range scheme for myself. I would never be content just teaching composition and service courses. I would have to find a research specialty and begin trying to publish some scholarly articles. By the same token, Colorado State University would probably expect the same thing and might urge me to begin working toward a PhD. The academic and career situations were clear and straightforward. The larger question was more abstract and philosophical: did we belong in southern Utah?

Early one Saturday morning, too early for most people to be out and about unless they were delivering newspapers or milk, I was taking a stroll. Or maybe it was a saunter. Either way, I rounded a corner not far from our brick mausoleum home and encountered an old man sweeping the gutter.

"Gonna turn the water in this mornin'," he said. "Thought I'd better get these leaves and such outta the gutter."

"Oh?" I said. "Turn the water in?"

"You're that kid they hired from Colorado, ain't ya?"

"That's me."

"Never heard that term, 'turnin' the water in'?"

"Sure, back on the farm. I wouldn't expect to see anybody doing it in town."

He finished flicking leaves from the gutter and beckoned for me to follow him. On the other side of his house he pointed to a rectangular opening in the curb.

I'd seen these curb gaps in Cedar City before. I'd even figured out that they had something to do with water. You don't grow up in Colorado without recognizing irrigation dams when you see them, especially if your grandfather was a beet farmer.

"Soon's it gets good and dark," your grandpap might say, "you scoot out and raise the boards on Johnson's irrigation dam. Just don't let nobody see you."

"Irrigation," the old neighbor guy confirmed. "Saturdays, they turn the water down my street. Should be along any time now."

Intrigued, I listened to his description of how it worked. When Cedar City was laid out, it seems, the pioneers planned things so that water could be diverted from Coal Creek and sent down the gutters of certain streets. Some of these street-side gutters were more like concrete troughs with flat bottoms. They could carry more water that way, but the sharp sides meant that parallel parking was a good way to remove your tires from their rims.

In several places per block residents could slide a board into two grooves and dam up the water. The water then backed up enough to flow through a curb opening and irrigate a vegetable garden. Every so often there would be clear, cold water flowing along in the gutter outside our house, but I had never paid much attention. We even had one of those gaps in the gutter, should we ever wish to grow some groceries.

Talk about a "green" idea.

There was a time when a town's residents took direct personal interest in keeping their local river clean and flowing. They needed it for livestock. It replenished the shallow wells where they got water for drinking and washing. It was a cheap source of irrigation, and unlike the water most of us city folk spray onto our grass, it didn't have to be sanitized, chlorinated, and fluoridated.

In the Cedar City plan the water that wasn't used would flow on through the system of gutters and drains and back into the river below town. People respected it. I don't remember ever seeing someone draining antifreeze into the gutters or using the gutters as a place to dispose of grass clippings. (I *did* see a cigarette butt floating down the gutter one afternoon. Before I could pick it up there was a terrific thunderclap and bolt of lightning and it was gone.)

"Heck of a system," I said to the old guy. "Back home it'd take years of lawsuits and millions in government grants to organize something like that."

"Them pioneers, they was a savvy bunch," he agreed.

We both stood there in the quiet morning, the man patiently waiting for the irrigation water to saturate his garden plot and the young college professor wondering about his future.

Back home in Colorado, my great-grandfather pioneered an irrigation scheme near Fort Morgan, a project that would capture water from the Bijou River and store it in the Bijou Reservoir. A half dozen of his relations took up farmsteads around the reservoir site. The problem was that the Bijou is what's known as an "intermittent" stream, meaning that Noah might have found water in it, and possibly Moses if he had wandered that far. But the Bijou project would wear out a generation of Works before they moved on. Grandfather moved on. My father moved even farther on. And when my time came, I also left home and went my way.

We didn't stick to one place the way the Mormon pioneers did. Mine was a family that picked up and moved. This neighbor I had recently met, he could stand there motionless, watching water run through an opening in the curb. Me, I was already fidgeting and shifting my weight from one foot to the other. Cedar City is a nice place, but not the place I wanted to spend the rest of my career in.

"Them pioneers," he repeated. "They knew what was what. You take that Lyman Plan that Brigham Young got started, up in Salt Lake."

"Lyman Plan?" I repeated.

The morning sun was beginning to show above the rooftops. At our feet a gentle gurgling announced the arrival of the irrigation water, which obediently turned through the curb opening to dampen the neighbor's bean plants.

"That's what they called it, the Lyman Plan for laying out the streets. Dunno why. You figured out the addresses yet?"

"Sure. We've been here nearly two years now."

What I didn't mention to my urban farmer friend was that it had taken every bit of those two years for me to "figure out" the Lyman Plan of street numbering in Utah. Thanks to Brigham Young's penchant for formality and organization, many towns in the state followed a uniform numbering system.

The Lyman Plan goes like this.

First find the center of town, which was dubbed the "center" in the previous century and therefore only locatable by asking an elderly native or by visiting the local museum or temple, which turns out to be the center anyway. The streets leading away to the south are called the East or West streets while streets leading away from the center toward the east or west are called the North or South streets.

Any questions thus far?

These streets are assigned numbers according to their distance away from the center, but the numbers are not in single digits. Rather, they are in increments of one hundred so that if you leave the center and begin driving south, you will *not* come to 1st Street and then 2nd Street and then 3rd street; instead, you will come to 100 South, 200 South, and 300 South in that order. This will continue until your petrol runs out and you have come to 20,000 South unless you've crossed a city boundary without realizing it, in which case you're back to 3000 North of some new place toward whose center you are now heading.

Similarly, if you go east from the center, you'll cross 100 East, 200 East, and so on unless you are in Salt Lake City, in which case you could start a block west of center and cross West Temple, Main Street, State Street, and then 200 West. The one thing you can count on is that if you are searching for someplace and its address is, for instance, Arty's Storm Window and Automatic Firearms Repair at 900 South 600 West, it will be nine streets south of the town center and six streets west of it. Unless it's on Bluebird Terrace or Sunrise Avenue, when all bets are off. To clarify things a bit more, you have two choices: you can either drive down (or up) the street you are on until you come to 600 West and then drive south to 900 South, or you can find 900 Street and drive east or west to 600.

The beauty of it is that you don't have to return to the center of town each time you need to find someone's house. If the street sign says 600 West on one side and 900 South on the side at right angles to the previously mentioned side, you already know you're either nine or six blocks from the town center. (To determine whether it is south or west, spit on your finger and hold it straight up. If moss forms on one side, that's north. If somebody stops to find out why your finger is in the air, ask them for directions.)

Utah, contrary to some opinions, is not flat. Therefore, to save motorists the embarrassment of driving off a cliff or coming face to face with a steep sand dune, highway engineers make streets that curve and bend around geological features. This plays hell with the grid system, since your 900 South Street is now running south when it should go east. In some towns—a town named Bountiful comes to mind—it might be renamed at that point and become (a miracle!) 1200 East Street. Or in the event of a subdivision builder who let his wife name the streets, Wisteria Boulevard.

As I said, it only took us about two years to accustom ourselves to the grid system, which is actually very efficient once you learn it. I remember how pleased we were when we had been invited to a (nonalcohol) party by some friends who lived at 450 South 500 West, and it took us less than an hour to figure out that they lived just down the block.

Oddly enough, I don't remember ever seeing a street named for Mister Lyman.

The neighbor irrigating his garden had jogged my brain into wondering if my whole academic future really had to take place in Cedar City. The more I thought about it, the more I began to see these patterns everywhere. I felt like that woman in Amy Lowell's poem saying, "Christ, what are patterns for?" I was young and fancied myself an intellectual. I could recite the plot lines of all of Chaucer's *Canterbury Tales* and interpret all of Browning's poems (OK, OK, *not* the one that has the line "pears without prickles" in it). I could understand Shakespeare's plays, for crying out loud. And yet here I stood in a corner of Utah feeling proud because I grasped the nuances of the street system.

Oh my heck.

It was Fred C. Adams, indirectly, who led to our leaving Cedar City. I think he would be proud to know it. Do you know how some people influenced you in ways you didn't recognize until years after? As an undergraduate or maybe in high school, Sharon read a book called *The Microbe Hunters* and it affected her so much that in a few years she found herself in an anatomy lab dissecting dogs and human cadavers. Me, I read a book called *The Scholar Adventurers* and from that time forward I could think of no greater quests than to go searching for some old piece of vellum that John Milton once blew his nose on.

Before getting to the influence of Fred Adams, let me tell you a story about a man who was a kind of positive/negative force in my professional life. His example was so negative, in other words, that it had a positive effect on me.

When I first began teaching as a graduate teaching assistant at Colorado State University, I had days when I thought it would make a swell career and then I had those other days when I wasn't so sure. Late one afternoon in the final semester of my GTA-ship I was witness to something that would come to haunt me every time I considered becoming a college professor.

I was standing at the curb just outside Old Main waiting for Sharon to pick me up so we could go home and do some necking. I was joined there by Max Stoner, who was also waiting for his wife to drive him home. Max had never been able to attain a PhD or MFA and was therefore doomed to spend his career in the sure and certain knowledge that he would never rise above the rank of assistant professor. That suited him, however, because he was a creative writer and a daydreamer and had no interest in research. He was a self-promoting poet, always phoning the local newspaper to announce he had a poem of six lines published in the *Sugar Beet Grower's Gazette* or something. It was rumored that his vita included the entry "Professor Stoner is listed in a major directory of scholars and leaders," which he wrote after discovering his name in the faculty phonebook.

Stoner came to the curb and stood there with bulging briefcase in hand, no doubt holding a load of student stories or poems that he was taking home to grade. Then after several minutes he appeared to have a thought. He turned, went back into Old Main, and I saw him heading up the stairway leading to the third floor and his office. He returned without the briefcase.

Another several minutes passed.

We chatted a bit. Then he abruptly turned, went back into the building again, up the stairs again, and returned carrying not one but *two* briefcases. He stood there in a contemplative daze, examining one and then the other, and I do think he would have made another trip upstairs had his wife not driven up at that point to collect him.

Sharon drove up a minute later. As I got in the car and buckled my seatbelt I kissed her on the cheek and said, "Whatever you do, don't let me become an English professor."

Yet here I was in southern Utah where persons such as Woolf and Braithwaite and Rowley and Plummer, not to mention the students, were conspiring to make me feel that I was a *very* promising young professor indeed and that the profession of professing was probably the finest one to follow. Or as Eugene Woolf said when I asked him why *he* kept teaching college literature, "It's the last refuge of sanity we have left in the world."

All very cozy, teaching there. And I would have stayed in that cozy place, save for one other set of influences upon my view of academia.

In the years when my alma mater was preparing to slough off its role as Colorado Agricultural and Mechanical College and take its place as Colorado's state university, the governors took pains to stock their intellectual larder with the best young brains available. As a result, despite CSU being known as "Moo U" and "Cow College," for six years I sat at the feet of professors whose own alma maters included Columbia, Northwestern, Yale, Stan-ford, Marquette, and Oxford—to name but a few. Each ranking member of the English department had attained a doctorate and a professorship through specialization. The youngest person to achieve full professor authored a book about *Moby Dick* that is still honored for the depth of its opaqueness. Specialization, I was brought up to believe, was the way to the top.

No doubt this was why my thesis committee approved my thesis proposal in which I proposed to examine not only one of the most obscure, least examined, least meritorious, miniscule movements in England's literary history, but one small poem written by one small opponent of that movement, a man who had satirized at least three promising poets into oblivion. My sole claim to employable expertise, in other words, was that I was on the way of becoming one of only two living scholars qualified to write about William Edmondstoune Aytoun and the Spasmodic School of Poetry.

It kind of takes your breath away, doesn't it?

Not only was Colorado calling us back, but I was also hearing the siren song of the academic podium, that concrete bunker of the intellectual ego from whence one could pontificate and take potshots at voids in human understanding. Ignorance being so rife among young Americans, a Dispenser of Truth and Wisdom would never run out of clients; better yet, college teaching was one of the few rackets going in which the customer is always *wrong*.

I convinced myself there was no room for a Victorian specialist at the College of Southern Utah. No doubt I could have achieved tenure as the Resident Token Gentile (I was very good at it, after all), but I needed to specialize, specialize, specialize. I felt I had nothing of lasting value to offer Southern Utah, and it had, alas, little to offer me except the chance to teach freshman composition, journalism, and vocabulary building for the rest of my life.

And that's how I get to Fred Adams. Whilst I was agonizing over specializations and future what-ifs, across campus there was another upward-bound young man of arts and letters who was not-so-quietly going about accomplishing exactly the caliber of thing I now wish I had accomplished.

I was not among Fred Adams's immediate circle of acquaintances. We had met, we recognized one another, and even spoke of Shakespeare together, but that was about it. Mr. Adams was a POT—Person of Theater—one of those people who, like young Will of Stratford, had been smitten by the spotlight. When old Will said "all the world's a stage," he meant it. To a certain kind of theater person, everywhere *is* a stage. Take a POT to the grocery store and they look first for the ticket booth and then decide whether they want to enter stage left (vegetables and frozen pizza) or stage right (cereal, laundry soap, and greeting cards).

Fred Adams took himself to Broadway for a few years, and while he might have made a considerable splash in New York if he had chosen to specialize in some "set" kind of acting role—specialized, if you will, in being the sneering cripple or the bewildered boyfriend—he thought he might be happier somewhere in a landscape with a bit more air and scenery. Thus he arrived in Cedar City. But before entirely settling in he washed out his shirts, repacked his valise, and headed for the big, famous Shakespeare festival of Ashland, Oregon.

What he brought back to Cedar City from Ashland was a dream, a vision that a replica of Will Shakespeare's Globe Theatre would one day rise out of the lawn on the campus of the College of Southern Utah. He visualized tourists stopping to see *The Taming of the Shrew* while on their way to Las Vegas or Reno. Even to this day travelers who are heading for the London Bridge at Havasu City can stop off in Cedar City and see a performance of *Much Ado About Nothing.*

More than once did Dr. Braithwaite meet me on campus and ask me to walk with him to the site chosen for Fred Adams's Globe Theatre replica. As Dr. Braithwaite spoke, my mind's eye could already see those half-timbered walls, those soft midsummer evenings made softer by the strains of medieval music, the faint smell of greasepaint on the air. For the faculty the project was a main topic of conversation. Townspeople and merchants described it to visitors. Money came from nowhere and from everywhere; encouragement came from the same community that had wanted my family to have a decent house and furniture.

A decade or so ago Sharon and I went back to Cedar City to see what Fred Adams had built. It was just as Dr. Braithwaite had said it would be. Incongruously, unbelievably, Adams's theater was a man's vision given substance, a dream realized in timber and mortar. We strolled through the lengthening evening across the campus toward what is now known as the Adams Shakespearean Theatre and walked into the magic.

After sundown in that corner of the campus the gatherings of spruce and fir seem to link branches in the dark to make towering shadows of the light from sidewalk lamps. Walks lead gently up and over little hills of lawn, curving among shrubbery. An evening coolness cleanses the air and brings the nostrils light reminders of cedar, piñon, mown grass, and flower beds. You pass through the pool of light under a sidewalk lamp and find yourself looking up at the medieval half-timbered wall of a theater. You see people in Shakespearean costume hawking fresh oranges, juggling jester's sticks, doing tumbling tricks for coins. Your ear is greeted by the strains of a quartet singing or a lute or flute being played. Inside, after dark stairs and passages, you emerge into open air again. Above the banks of seats the stars make points in the jet black sky. The little stage below you is about to become Venice or a fantastic island or the battlefield of Agincourt.

I said that I didn't know Fred Adams all that well. I didn't know if he'd been punished in school for not listening to Chaucer's prologue, I didn't know if he ever took a glass of wine, nor did I know whether he drank coffee. I don't know if he went to temple, was an elder of the LDS church, or even if he belonged to it. What I *do* know is that when you open your latest copy of Bartlett's *Familiar Quotations* to the page containing Joseph Campbell's famous line, "follow your bliss," there ought to be a picture of Adams and his theater next to it.

"And I will give it unto you . . . if you seek it with all your hearts" (Doctrine and Covenants 38:19).

As it happened, I followed that selfsame advice.

Back at Colorado State University, Professors Stimmel and Henry (acting as co-chairmen after the abdication of King Rex Nostrum) offered me the honor of teaching three sections of freshman composition and one of introduction to literature. It was my opening, my chance to become a superspecialized pedagogue on his way toward being a fully fledged tenured professor.

A new chairman came along, together with a new set of "rules" stipulating that all faculty must hold PhDs. No exceptions. If you weren't a doctor of philosophy, you'd better get out and get to be one. My fellow instructors who had nothing but six years of higher education and two degrees to qualify them to teach comma splices and dangling modifiers suddenly needed to enroll in PhD programs. Some tried doing it by mail, only to discover that the administration tended to look somewhat askance at a doctorate that had been "earned" in three weeks and cost less than $200. Others enrolled at the nearest school offering a PhD of any sort—a doctorate of home economics in English or a doctorate of English and kindergarten teaching techniques looked pretty good considering that classes only met once a week.

Sharon and I considered the University of Nebraska where the English department had offered to let me into their linguistics program on probation. Linguistics was not my "bliss" by any means, but there were more jobs going in linguistics than in literature. I drove out to interview at Lincoln and drove home in a blizzard. Nebraska, it turns out, is almost without windbreaks and is much closer to the Arctic Circle than to the equator.

I was pretty good at imagining stuff, but I could not imagine spending winters in Nebraska. Nor, to be honest, could I imagine spending two years studying linguistics. Farewell to a career of examining the declension of the expletive "duh!" from Anglo Saxon to the present day and farewell, too, to the eternal blizzards of *baja* Dakota. We opted for my second choice, Albuquerque. It's harder to spell than "Lincoln," but in Albuquerque the residents brag about recipes for green chile, not about how many sets of snow tires they've gone through.

And so it was that I did my UNM doctorate (in record time) and returned to Colorado State University expecting accolades for furthering my expertise in the subject of Spasmodic poets of Victorian England. The lack of applause was deafening.

Undeterred, I worked my feet down into the clay for a foothold, took a deep breath, and plunged in. I wrote articles, began to outline my first book, and started the long process of sucking up to administrators. One day I was asked if I would "mind" teaching a course in Western American literature even though it was far outside my specialty.

Being a good suck up, I said "sure." And "sure" led me to begin reading some of the most challenging, interesting literature I had ever encountered. The mythic complexity of Western American literature was stunning. And when I realized—with a physical jolt—that Frank Waters's *The Man Who Killed the Deer* and *People of the Valley* were deeply Jungian, I was hooked. Who were these critics, these writers? What poets, what forces? What the hammer, what the chain . . . (Sorry, William Blake took over for a moment there.) But in the immortal words of either Butch Cassidy or the Sundance Kid when they saw that the posse was still behind them, "Who *are* these guys?"

I had changed majors four times in college, and now, almost ten years after earning my doctorate, damned if I didn't go and do it again. After reinventing myself in Western American literature I enjoyed the honor of being chosen president of the Western Literature Association and managed to publish a major anthology of Western prose and poetry.

One day I found myself walking across the CSU campus with George Dennison, one of the university's top administrators. We were near South Hall, which is one of the oldest buildings on campus. Its ancient brick walls face a big lawn bordered by big spruce and elms.

"Why don't we use South Hall for a Western American Studies Center?" I asked.

"To do what?"

"Set up a major for studying all about the West. History, literature, climatology, geology, botany—turn out students who could go to work for any company doing business in the West. We could have a research library there in South Hall. Out here on the lawn, right where everyone driving College Avenue would see it, we'd have an outdoor museum with American Indian lodges, irrigation flumes, cattle, and cowboy exhibits, sugar beet exhibits, geology dioramas—it could be a tourist attraction."

"Quite a dream," he said. "I'll see what I can do. Put it in writing."

I put it in writing. I got a half dozen chairmen to sign on and agree to allow Western Studies majors into upper level classes in botany, geology, and history, not to mention business and literature. The languages chairman said he'd start a special class in regional Spanish for Western Studies majors. Two vice presidents endorsed the idea.

However, when George Dennison left for a much better job elsewhere, my scheme soon died. The administrator who replaced him was "too new" to "sign on" to any kind of "special interest" project. Another department wanted to seize South Hall and modernize it into offices. I thought about Fred C. Adams back there at College of Southern Utah and wondered how he had done it. How had he created Shakespeare's theater on that campus? What did he have that I didn't have?

I was mowing the front yard one day when two young men wearing white shirts and dark neckties came pedaling up the street. They asked if they could park their bikes in the shade while they canvassed the cul-de-sac.

Another confession: there was a time when the sight of an approaching missionary, witness, deacon, emissary, or spokesperson would have made me dash inside the house and reply to the doorbell with my imitation of a rabid Rottweiler.

"Grrr, rowf! Hungry dog! Rabies! Grrr, rowf. Go away!"

But it was a soft, long-shadowed afternoon. There was a faint perfume of roses on the air, and somewhere in the distance there was a light strain of music.

"We're on a mission to let people know about the Church of Latter-day Saints," one of the young men said.

"Come sit in the shade," I replied. "Tell me all about it."

CPSIA information can be obtained at www.ICGtesting.com
Printed in the USA
241655LV00001B/3/P

9 780806 141947